COPP
IN
DEEP

COPP IN DEEP

BY
DON PENDLETON

DONALD I. FINE, INC.
NEW YORK

Library of Congress Cataloging-in-Publication Data

Pendleton, Don.
  Copp in Deep

  I. Title.
PS3566.E465C65   1989   813'.54   88-46165
ISBN 1-55611-141-X

Manufactured in the United States of America

10 9 8 7 6 5 4 3 2 1

Designed by Irving Perkins Associates

For Linda—
who keeps reminding me
how sweet life can be...
and proves it day by day.

COPP IN DEEP

CHAPTER
ONE

HE LOOKED seven feet tall and at least half that wide, lean and mean with nasty eyes and cruel lips, a fist the size of my head— and I knew that this guy was going to give me more trouble than I could afford at such an embarrassing moment. So I let him get just close enough for a little pop with the stun gun. That changed his intentions, but only for a moment. He stood there at the corner of the desk like Frankenstein with rigor mortis, trying to shake it off, and I could see the control settling back into those murderous eyes so I gave him a few more volts. That one did it. He went down like a tall tree in the forest and took every- thing on the desk with him. But alarms were ringing all over the joint by now and I knew that I was in for a hell of a time. The Dobermans would be turned loose and the whole building sealed like a tomb before I could even get moving. There was only one

9

way out, and it was not a very cheerful way, but I took it. I heaved a chair through that second story window and went out close behind it without even looking first. Whatever was out there could be no worse than what was waiting for me inside. I was in the dumbest place in the world and probably for a dumb reason—a KGB headquarters, for God's sake—so it would serve me right to meet a dumb fate.

Don't wonder why a small-time private cop was burglarizing a Soviet consulate in the small of the night and playing commandoes with their KGB; I had enough wonder for all of us, and I still don't know what possessed me to get into something like that. Well, okay, maybe I do know, but it's going to take a while to explain it in a believable way—and maybe I can't even do that if you are one of those who think that *glasnost* and *perestroika* mean that the Russian bear is really only a playful cub with lovable intentions.

I can tell you firsthand that it ain't so, and I have the scars to prove it—but I guess I'd better just give you the whole story and let you decide for yourself. Just don't fault my literary style, as some have already done. Understand right up front that I'm a cop, I've always been a cop, I was even born a Copp—I think like a cop, eat like one, love like one—so okay, I write like a cop, that is what you are going to get here. I'll try not to offend anyone's literary sensibilities but I can give it to you only the way it came at me and I wouldn't bother telling you about it if it was not a really wild story.

It's about spies and counterspies, cops and robbers, patriots and traitors, driven men and fascinating women, booze and sex and drugs and pornography, greed and avarice and the selling of a country, politics and corruption and murder, heroism and cowardice—life behind the scenes, as it comes to play in the USA of today—and we'll try to sort it all out the way I had to as I experienced it: Joe Copp in deep shit.

Ready for that? Okay. Welcome to my shitty world. Here's the way it started...

OM CHASE called me at home late on Sunday night and I knew he was in trouble just by the way he spoke my name. Tom and I were partners years ago when we were both with LAPD, so of course we'd been through a lot together and I still considered him a close friend although we hadn't seen each other face to face for several years and even the phone calls were not that frequent. You know how it is when people go separate ways in life. You mean to keep in touch but you get so caught up in mere survival that the finer things just sort of slip away from you and sometimes it just seems impossible to do all the things that need doing, like keeping in touch with old friends even when it's inconvenient to do so.

Tom had left the department about the same time I did, he into the private sector as a security consultant and me still trying to find some place to be a cop the way I believe it should be done. I spent five years straitjacketed with the sheriff's department while Tom went on to ever bigger and better things. At the time this all started, he was chief of security for one of the big defense contractors and we had been totally out of touch for about a year. The last time I'd talked to him, in fact, was the day I opened my agency and he called to wish me well.

This time I knew it was no casual call. Tom has always been cool and unflappable on the surface but he gets a telltale little stricture of the vocal chords when he's uptight about something. That's how I knew he was in trouble the minute I picked up the phone.

"Joe?"

"Kiss my ass, I can't believe it, but it sounds like Missing Tom Chase. It's a hell of a time to call, pal."

"I know. I'm sorry. Are you alone?"

I looked regretfully at the vacant pillow beside me as I replied, " 'Fraid so."

"I need to talk to you, Joe. Seriously. Listen, I'm just at the bottom of your hill, corner of Sierra Madre. I—"

"Great, come on up. I'll put the coffee on."

"No. I think I shouldn't. I could be under surveillance. Could you meet me down here?"

I was coming wide awake now and reaching for a cigarette. Trying to quit, but…"Okay. Where?"

"Self-serve gas station on the southwest corner. You still driving the old Cad?"

"Yeah."

"Okay. Pull in to a pump and start filling up. I'll find you."

"Look for me in five minutes," I told him, and got moving immediately.

I actually made it in about four, dressed sloppily but quickly in a sweat suit and sneakers. It was a 24-hour combination gas station and convenience store which I use frequently, and I'd just placed the nozzle in the fill-tube of my car when a white Chrysler pulled in at the opposite side of the pump. Tom delayed a moment inside his car, opening and closing a couple of doors and fiddling with something in the glove box, then he got out of the Chrysler and walked past me without a glance my way as he went to the cashier's window to pre-pay his purchase.

I was still playing with my nozzle when he returned and began playing with his. He made an affable small-talk comment about the price of gas and we jawed on for a moment the way strangers will at a gas pump, then he declared in a voice I could barely hear, "I'm putting you on a thousand a day plus expenses but it's strictly under the table and it's just between you'n me.

The package is under your car, driver's side. Don't call or try to see me, and don't mention my name to anyone. I'll contact you for reports and further instructions. Don't let me down, Joe. This is really heavy."

I hung up my nozzle, got back in the Cad, reached down and pulled in a nine-by-twelve manila envelope, and took off without a backward glance—and I didn't look inside the envelope until I was sitting at my own kitchen table with freshly brewed coffee in hand.

Even that initial look seemed like pretty heavy stuff, yeah. For starters, there were copies of several classified documents in that envelope. One of them outlined the loose parameters of an FBI "sting" operation that had been in place for several months in the local area, involving the sale of military secrets by civilian employees of government contractors—of which there are many in the Los Angeles area.

Another classified document seemed to be an informal report from an unidentified FBI informant having to do with the movements and activities of several high executives of Tom's company.

A third document was an official FBI history and profile of Tom Chase himself, several pages in length.

There was other stuff—glossy black-and-white photos and brief biographical sketches of the same men named in the FBI report—another envelope containing fifty $100 bills—and a complete roster of management-level personnel at Tom's company.

I was staring gloomily at the stack of money when the phone rang and again Tom Chase was in my ear.

"Had time to look it over?" he asked without chummy preamble.

I said, "Yeah. It's out of my league, pal. What the hell am I supposed—?"

"Joe," he cut in urgently, "I've got no one else to turn to. I think I'm being watched night and day and I don't even know who my friends are anymore. I think they've got a mole in my own office. Worse, I'm afraid I may even have some kinky executives on my hands and I don't know how high it goes so I don't know who to take it to. They—"

"Take it to the feds," I suggested. "That's where it belongs."

"It's already there," he said, "and that's what is driving me wild. I think we've got some kinky feds here too!"

I said, "Well hell, Tom . . ."

"No, I mean it. I think this sting may have turned into a coverup looking for patsies. Guess who is shaping up as Patsy Number One."

I said, "If you're clean, Tom . . ."

"Don't give me that," he said in a voice almost totally shut down. "You know damn well I'm clean. Look, I want to hire you. The five grand is a retainer and—"

"You don't have to—"

"No, bullshit, I do have to, and I'll get it all back from the company once we clear it up. I want you to drop anything else you might be doing and get right onto this, the Joe Copp way. You know what I mean. Damn the torpedoes and don't worry about sensitive toes. Go wherever you have to go and do whatever you have to do but, goddammit, find out exactly what is going on with these people and do it quick."

I tried to get out of it. I really did. I told my old partner, "I don't even know where to start, pal."

"Start at the Russian consulate."

"Oh sure."

"The KGB station chief there is a guy named Gudgaloff." He spelled it, then told me, "He's their top man in the region. Even the consul general at San Francisco reports to him. A tight network of agents work out of this office, some in the local emigré community and a few operating in the highest circles in this town. I'm talking high society and high finance, high government, all of it. If you could get a list of those people..."

I said, "Sure," but meant, "no way."

Tom took it both ways and assured me, "You can if anyone can, so..."

"What good would a list do you?" I wondered, still thinking about it.

"Someone on that list could be right here in my own company, in a very high position."

"I see," I said, but I didn't see anything. "How do you know all this stuff, pal?"

"It's my business to know it."

"You have a working liaison with the local FBI people?"

"Sure."

"Wouldn't they be interested in such a list?"

"Sure, but..."

"But you don't trust them."

"Let's just say I don't know who to trust." There was a long silence, then: "Joe..."

"I'm here."

"I'm not all that clean, I guess. I mean morally, yeah, I'm clean as a whistle... but technically, uh, I think I may have been used without realizing it. I may have passed some stuff."

I growled, "Jesus, Tom..."

"I know. I should've known, but how could I know? How would anyone know? I think maybe I was set up."

"To take a fall?"

"To take the fall, yeah. Now I don't know which way to turn. And it gets really sticky because..."

"Because?"

"Miriam."

That is his wife. Nice girl. Never really got to know her well because he married her just before he left the department and, as I've said, we had not been really close since that time.

"What are you saying, Tom?"

"Maybe I was set up by a woman."

So now I got it. I sighed and told him, "Call me again in the morning. I'll skull it, and if I think I can do anything to earn your money..."

"Forget that, Joe," he said urgently. "The money doesn't mean a thing. I'm getting strung up here, pal."

When an old friend puts it that way...

I sighed again and told him, "Call me at eight."

He did, and I agreed to look into it, and that is how I came to be in the Russian consulate on that Tuesday night with Ivan the Terrible breathing fire on my neck.

But that was just the beginning.

So far I was into it only about ankle deep. Before I could begin to comprehend that small depth, I would be into it clear to the chin and sinking fast.

CHAPTER
TWO

ACTUALLY I did not start at the consulate. I spent most of Monday doing a make on Tom's company and its key executives in the area. Wasn't all that difficult because it is one of the largest outfits in the industry, a major force in that "military-industrial complex" that President Eisenhower used to be so worried about. Eisenhower must be spinning in his grave these days because the largest defense budget during his years in office was under fifty billion dollars, according to the figures I found, and the recent build-up under Reagan already exceeds a trillion bucks. A trillion is a very big number, you know. To get there, you start by counting to a thousand a thousand times. That only gets you a million. Then it takes a thousand millions to get to a billion and another thousand billions to get you a trillion. That's a damn lot of money. For the average working stiff in this country who's dragging down around thirty grand a year, he'd have to work thirty three million years to get there. Even if you earned a million a year it would take a million years to reach a trillion dollars. See, you can't get there. But our government gets there every year or two, and much of that goes to the defense contractors.

I give you that because there is a rule that says that big bucks always attract big crimes and I want to be sure that you are with me on this. It may not be true that every man has his price but I'd have to bet that most of us do. There's the joke about a guy who crashes this big society party in Washington and right away he's dancing with the hostess, this top socialite. He asks her if she'd go to bed with him for a million dollars. She laughs, takes it as a joke, and says of course she would. So he keeps whittling her down—would she do it for a thousand, for a hundred and so on. Finally she tires of the joke at fifty bucks and indignantly replies, "Young man, just what do you think I am!" So he tells her, "Madam, we've already established what you are. Now we're just dickering about price."

See? As the price goes up, morals go down. Take it from a cop with eighteen years on the streets, that's a rule. And I was looking for something that would explain why things had become so bad in this country that our FBI had to set up floating sting operations to find people willing to sell our vital secrets to potential enemies. As the socialite was a whore, see, these people are traitors—just waiting for a price.

A trillion bucks, I guess, would bring a lot of them out of the woodwork—whores and traitors alike—and the hell of it is that many of these could be people you'd never suspect to go that way. I was looking for a handle to the thing, trying to get a policeman's feel for the forces that convert loyal citizens into traitors, and that trillion bucks in the defense budget seemed to be a good enough place to start, with Tom's employer at the focal point. Not that there is a direct link between the defense budget and the price of a traitor, but with that much money in play you have to know that all the human frailties are going to be put to the test as the pie is being cut.

I'll call the company "PowerTron," and tell you that if I used the real name you'd recognize it instantly. It's one of the biggies in the business with fingers in all of the defense pies and annual revenues into the several billions of dollars in California alone. The Los Angeles division of the company had been fined repeatedly in recent years for contract abuses and some of its key management figures accused of kickback deals involving Pentagon officials and subcontractors.

It seemed a good place to start, yeah. Even the largest company in the world is, for all its corporate dignity and prestige, still no more than a collection of highly competitive people all working for a price, and the things they are willing to do for their price must increase as the price increases. If the lady is a whore at a million bucks then she's a whore at heart, and the same goes for these so-called white-collar criminals whose only game is win and whose only sin is lose. If they'll steal from their country for one reason they'll steal again for another, with little more than opportunity and reward deciding the name of the game.

So the name of this game was *treason* and I was looking for players. You don't solve crimes, you uncover criminals—that was my particular game and I had good enough reason to believe that I knew it fairly well. I was about to learn that I still had a lot to learn.

Morris Putnam was a VP at PowerTron, in charge of finances. He was 52 years old, held degrees in both law and accounting, was married with three kids in college, had a nice place in the hills above Pasadena, been with the company for sixteen years. He was caught cheating three times in the past year by the GAO but each time it was another poor sucker under him who took the blame for the "errors" and got sacked. Putnam was the darling of the board of directors and was considered to be next in line as CEO.

George Delancey, another Veep, was in charge of contract administration. He was only forty but a rising star with PowerTron, a mere two years out of the Pentagon as a civilian procurements officer, and it shows the corporate mindset here when you know that Delancey left Washington under a cloud and barely escaped indictment over irregularities in his procurement programs. Gordon Maxwell, a retired brigadier general and chairman of PowerTron, couldn't sign this guy up fast enough, which shows also how insider influence is valued and rewarded when billion dollar contracts are at stake.

I put all this in the record at this point because these are principal players and this is the basic setting for this story. We'll be moving away from it at lightspeed in just a moment and I want you to understand for sure where it all began. It began in venal minds in an atmosphere of governmental corruption and corporate sleaze. Remember that. And remember that treason, as it is most often encountered at home these days, is just another exercise of the criminal instinct. In this case, it was also quite a refinement of it.

YOU DON'T have to be a cloak-and-dagger guy to get away with it, any good second-story man would find the place a piece of cake. I went in at just a few minutes before the close of business hours, signed in at the front desk and asked to see the attaché for cultural affairs. I also handed over one of my bogus business cards identifying me as a movie and television producer, and it played very well—maybe because a lot of business had been going down between Hollywood and Moscow of late. I was sent right up. Didn't go all the way up though, only to the roof of the automatic elevator cage, and I came prepared for a long stay in that elevator shaft. Don't know if anyone ever missed their Hollywood producer or if anyone looked for him. The cage made about a dozen trips up and down during the first couple of hours then settled at ground level and stayed there until I bailed out just past midnight.

The building had been quiet as a tomb for hours when I slipped back through the manhole and sent the cage to the second floor. I programmed it to go on to the top and to stop at each floor along the way, just in case someone was watching the indicators in the lobby, but I guess even that little touch was unnecessary.

Nothing was stirring on the second floor. Gudgaloff's office was locked but the door yielded quickly and quietly with the gentlest persuasion and I had twenty good minutes in there before Ivan came along, apparently on a routine check of the building—plenty of time to rifle the desks and file cabinets. Actually I could have done it in about a minute because the little black book was waiting for me in the first drawer I opened. It looked too easy so I kept searching for other bits and pieces—and came up with quite a bit, in fact.

All the stuff was tucked away and I was ready to call it a night when the big guy came lumbering in. He didn't seem startled or even surprised to see me there, just went straight for my head and he would have had it in one massive hand on the first lunge if my reflexes had been one shade off. I evaded the grab and went straight for my equalizer, a neat little nonlethal device no larger than a flashlight. It packs 47,000 volts of stunning energy and could stop a charging buffalo in its tracks. As I think I mentioned earlier, I had to hit this guy twice to take him down, and by now the commotion had alerted the nightwatch and alarms were ringing all over the building.

Tom had given me a detailed verbal layout of the place and its security apparatus so I knew pretty much what I was up against. I knew there was no way out if I should get caught in the act. The plan had been to spend the night in the elevator shaft and make a casual exit the next day, hopefully unnoticed among the other visitors, and I had every reason to believe that I could pull it off successfully.

But now...well, as I said earlier, there was no other way—so I took the only exit possible. Sometimes, I think, I have an angel on my shoulder and this must have been one of those times because I went through that window with absolutely no expectation of a successful landing. It was just a wild-ass act of total desperation—sort of like saying, "Okay, God, here's your chance to get me for all the fuckups all these years," and instead He reaches out with a soft hand and an indulgent smile.

I went through some kind of an umbrella-shaped tree, or maybe one of those giant California shrub things like oleander, maybe, with many slender branches and leathery leaves. Whatever, it cushioned my fall and I came down feetfirst through one side of this thing astride several yielding branches and hit the ground running, much to my surprise, with nothing broken but scratches everywhere.

It's a corner building and sits right on the streets, no grounds, no walls, so I was back in America in one leap and home free if I could just keep moving. Nobody was shooting at me, no dogs were nipping at my scratched ass, and I couldn't hear any approaching sirens, so I figured my chances were pretty good for a clean break.

But this car screeches away from the curb about a half a block away as I am crossing the street, and it's coming at me full tilt. I've got nowhere to go now, see—it's just the street and the sidewalks and tall buildings to either side—so I haul out my old blunderbuss, a Smith & Wesson model 57, and I'm lining up in firing stance to meet that charge when the car does a sudden one-eighty on smoking tires and rocks to a halt. This incredibly pretty woman with Siamese cat eyes throws a door open and yells at me, "Come on!"

I'm just standing there wondering what the hell, one eye over my shoulder toward the consulate and the other trying to figure the woman. Then I see the fucking dogs coming around the corner like straight out of hell—biggest goddamned Dobermans I've ever seen, I think four of them, having the time of their lives—and the mental debate ends right there.

The car was moving again even before I got there. I dove inside about four G's and that whole scene was far behind before I could get straightened around and upright in the seat.

"That was close," she said coolly, one eye on the rearview mirror.

I was breathing too hard to reply, but I had nothing particularly cunning to say anyway.

It was a safe harbor, I hoped—for a moment—and God himself couldn't have sent me a prettier pilot.

But this lady was a lot more than that.

CHAPTER
THREE

YEAH, SHE worked for old pal Tom Chase but insisted that he knew nothing about her presence outside that consulate. Something had "gone wrong" and there was no one else to send, so she'd taken it on herself to backstop my play. Said she'd been out there less than an hour when the second-story window shattered and things came flying out of it, had no idea I was one of those things until she saw me limp into the street, figured then she'd better close fast and lend aid.

I was entirely grateful for that, since I had not decided to change my name and fate to Alpo.

"What went wrong?" I asked her.

"Tom was arrested," she replied, without even a glance my way.

"Arrested for what?"

"Espionage."

I said, "Oh God."

She said, "He'd intended to back you up but the FBI came for him just as he was leaving for the stakeout."

"What time was that?"

"Little after ten," she said coolly. "He told me you'd be especially vulnerable for the first hour after midnight, so...did you get it?"

"Get what?"

"What you went to get."

I shrugged, decided to play a little dumb, told her, "Not sure what I got. Bits and pieces mostly."

She was getting fidgety. "Did you find Nicky's book?"

"Whose book?"

"Wasn't your assignment to find Nicholas Gudgaloff's networking book?"

I smiled, purely for my own benefit because she hadn't looked directly at me once from the minute I entered her car. "I don't know from assignments," I told her. "Just doing a favor for a friend—or didn't he tell you that?"

"I know that you were policemen together." She had a curious accent, just barely, a very light touch of something that I couldn't quite pigeonhole. I supposed that it could sound very nice under the proper circumstances. At the moment, she was coming cold and distant—as though she either didn't like me or didn't trust me, maybe both. That was okay because I didn't entirely trust her either, and I hadn't yet made up my mind if I liked her.

"Nicky, huh," I said thoughtfully.

"All his friends call him that."

"And you are one of those."

"Of course, or so he thinks. What's the matter with you?"

"Whattaya mean?"

"Are you on board, or not?"

"On board what?"

She was beginning to sound very perplexed. We were just driving aimlessly around the town until it seemed safe to return to the general vicinity of the scene of the crime. My car was parked a block over from the consulate, and it had not seemed advisable to try to pick it up while fleeing the area.

"On board what?" I asked again.

"Never mind," she replied coldly. "Give me the evidence and I will take you to your car."

I said, "No dice, kid. I got it for Tom, I'll give it to Tom."

"You can't do that now!" she cried. "Don't you understand? He's been arrested!"

"So I'll turn it over to his lawyer," I told her.

She was mad as hell now and starting to drive that way. "I am the only friend he has left," she said, emphasizing each word and now tossing me angry glances as she sped recklessly along the deserted street. "Give me the evidence so that I may develop the case for him. Otherwise..."

"Yeah?"

"Otherwise there is no hope."

"*No* hope?"

"*No* hope, that is what I said."

"It's that bad?"

"Yes. Will you give me the evidence?"

"I'll think about it," I told her. I was hurting like hell, all over, and this kid was doing nothing for me. Okay, so maybe I was taking the pain out on her when I should have been licking her all over in gratitude, but what the hell...? Things were happening too fast.

I said, "Take a right at the next corner, but slowly. I parked a block north, just look for the prettiest car on the street."

"We must settle this first," she said stubbornly, but she did slow and take the turn I'd requested.

"It's already settled," I told her. "I'll keep the stuff until Tom tells me from his own mouth what to do with it. It's the Cadillac, next block. Drop me and—huh-uh, keep on going, be cool and keep on going, don't look at the guy."

I had spotted another car parked on the cross street just below the Cad, hell, it was nearly one o'clock in the morning and here's this car parked nowhere with a guy sitting in it doing nothing but peering at passing cars. We passed another at the next crossing and still a third idling on the ramp of a closed parking garage and ready to roll on instant notice.

"What is it?" she asked anxiously.

"My car is staked out," I told her. "And those aren't Russians, they're L.A. city cops. So what the hell is going down here, lady?"

She looked scared for the first time, definitely flustered. "I don't know what it means," she assured me. "But I'm sure Tom didn't..."

"Didn't what?"

"Break already. How could the police know about you?"

"How could anybody?"

"Indeed."

Indeed, sure. I get it later that her name is Gina Terrabona. Don't ask what kind of name that is, I have no idea—sounds sort of Italian, doesn't it, but she told me that she was American-born to an American father and Israeli mother. The marriage failed a few years after she was born and her mother returned to Israel and took Gina with her. She grew up over there, educated there, served in the Israeli army and worked in military intelligence, came back to this country and claimed her birthright as an American citizen, worked at the Pentagon for a while—again in intelligence—got the job with PowerTron through her Washington connections.

See, this is all starting to sound too damn squirrely and I am starting to wonder if I am caught up in Tom Chase's weird idea of a practical joke. Meanwhile I am scratched and bruised all over, I think maybe I have a wrenched back and definitely a tender ankle, and my head is beginning to throb.

The kid is starting to fall apart. She's crying silently and her knuckles are white she's gripping the wheel so hard. I'm feeling like an ungrateful bastard but still I'm clinging to the hostility I'm feeling deep down inside somewhere and I am wondering what in the hell I am doing in this fucking mess. I'm a private cop, for God's sake, and maybe my license to make a living that way is on the line—forget that, maybe my freedom to sleep where I want and eat what I want is on the line. It was all for nothing anyway, the goddam guy was guilty as sin—always knew he was too ambitious for his own good, and then that wife of his just made it doubly worse. If she didn't want to be a cop's wife then why the hell did she marry a cop?—it's dumb, he went crazy for that snooty little bitch and sold out his country and now he's sold me out—he was in jail and I was going to be right beside him—Jesus Christ, an accomplice to espionage!—I couldn't believe this shit!

I told the sniveling kid from Israel, "Get ahold of yourself, God dammit, and get ahold of this car too! You're weaving all over the God damned...aw shit—forget it, forget it—look, we'll work this out. Don't cry, dammit, we'll work it out!"

She really did have great eyes. Like I said, Siamese-cat eyes—you know that color?—and set into the head sort of that way, too, real slanty, but not an Oriental look, I mean not a human Oriental look but like the cat—and that skin as smooth as silk and just begging to be touched.

So maybe I'm a jerk and I would let Mata Hari herself walk

away free if she dropped a couple of tears my way, but I really had no reason to be shitty with this kid, not yet anyway, and I did have a lot to thank her for. It was a damn gutsy thing she did for me back there with the hounds at my heels, and I hadn't even thanked her.

"I don't know what to do!" she wailed.

Well, hell, neither did I.

But I patted her arm in what was meant to be a comforting way and told her, "Just go home. I'll handle it. Trust me. I'll handle it."

"Where will you go? For now, I mean? You can't go to your car. And if they are watching your car..."

Yeah, I got that. I couldn't go home, either. Shit, I didn't know where I could go. Blind, maybe.

But I'm a guy, see—I'm big and I'm tough when I need to be—and there's a certain image to maintain, for us guys. So I just shrugged and told her, "Don't worry it. I've been here before. I'll be here again. Meanwhile..."

"Come home with me," she said quietly.

I didn't give it a second thought. I just said, "Okay."

But it wasn't okay. Not at all. It was sheer hell.

A guy was waiting for her in her apartment. She spotted the crack of light at the bottom of the door and whispered to me, "I left no lights on."

So I took the key from her and pushed her clear, unleathered the 57 and let it lead me inside.

The son of a bitch fired first, without warning, and with a bit too much fingerjerk to the pull. His bullet hit the wall beside my head and already I was reflexing the reply. The big round hit him squarely at center-chest and punched him backwards into a chair.

He was dead before I could touch him with my hands.

Fairly nice looking guy, well dressed, about my age.

"Do you know him?" I asked the Israeli.

She shook her head in mute, wide-eyed response.

So I went for the pockets, found his wallet, found a second wallet—a very familiar looking second wallet—opened it, and it was my turn to go mute and wide-eyed.

Talk about "deep," pal.

I had just shot to death a Special Agent of the FBI.

CHAPTER
FOUR

THERE WAS no search warrant that I could find and nothing appeared out of place in the apartment. The credentials found on the body identified the dead man as Walter Mathison and if the address on the driver's license was current he lived in Burbank and he was 38 years old. So, dammit, that probably meant a widow and kids left behind and it all seemed too damned pointless at the moment.

I heard sounds of voices in the hall as I was examining the scene, stepped out quickly because I knew what it was—two big guns had been fired in that building and it is not the sort of thing that goes unnoticed in the middle of the night. A man and a woman were standing in front of the next apartment, both dressed for the bedroom and talking excitedly until they saw me.

Then both clammed up real quick and were giving me the scared look, so I yelled down, "Did you hear it?"

The man nervously yelled back, "Sounded like a gun, didn't it."

I said, "There were some kids on the street just outside when I came up, dorking around. Probably them. Fireworks or something."

"Sounded like an M-80," the guy agreed.

"I'll call the police just to be sure," I volunteered.

The woman smiled at me and went back into her apartment. The guy waved and hurried back to his. He encountered another couple in an open doorway along the way and paused to reassure them.

Didn't do much for me, though.

Nor for the Israeli Kid.

She was white and trembly and fighting tears when I went back inside. "He was waiting here to kill me," she declared in a shaky voice.

"Why would he want to do that?" I asked her.

"I do not know why. But it is obvious, is it not?"

"Doesn't sound like the FBI way," I told her, "but these days we never know, so . . ."

Look, I was scared as hell, make no mistake. Even if the guy had gone renegade and had been playing some personal game of his own, not a fed alive would buy into a self-defense plea unless there was overwhelming evidence to support it. I had no evidence at all, of anything. And yeah, I was plenty scared. And maybe the kid was right, he'd come there to kill her. If so, were there others just like him? Tom Chase apparently thought so. So where the hell did that leave anything? What kind of crazy weave was I caught in?

Maybe Tom himself was kinky, this kid was kinky, and they'd been caught playing footsies with "Nicky" and the KGB. So maybe I'd been sucked in to interfere in a legitimate federal investigation and I'd just killed one of the investigators. Apparently I had even been turned to LAPD, maybe they'd known all along about the plan to heist the consulate, maybe they'd been watching me even before...

See, that's where my head was at and that is where my guts were at. Not exactly panic but cold clawing fear, to be sure. I have a clean record, understand, and I have friends in the police establishments of this area—even know a couple of feds on friendly terms—but there has been a cloud over my head all the time I've been a cop, followed me from job to job and even into the private sector, and the cloud says that Joe Copp is trouble looking for a place to happen. Don't know how I ever got such a rep because that really is not me. What I am really is a pussy cat and always a soft touch for a sob story—well, to a point—and I never believed that a policeman's job should be fully defined in any book. If you're a cop, dammit, then you're a cop all the time, in every circumstance, with every person. The cop is there to make a society work. Society is made up of people. A cop is part of that people, like white blood cells in a living body, and a good cop always responds appropriately to any attack upon that body. So sometimes there is no time to sit down with a textbook to find a proper response. You just have to do it—quickly, decisively, always with the best intentions, and with a little heart sometimes.

That's the way I cop.

Sometimes it gets me in trouble.

But I had never been in trouble like this before. And yeah, I was really scared.

ON TOP of everything else, it seems that I had taken on the
care and feeding of a homeless waif, one evicted by practical necessity and totally vulnerable to whatever may be
coming down the pike toward her. She had no family in
this country that she knew of, no friends whom she could trust
under the circumstances, and she was scared out of her skull.
So we rounded up some of her things and tossed them into a
small bag and I took her the hell out of there with me. I knew a
place near the high desert where one could hibernate for a while
in comfort and safety; what the hell, I couldn't just walk away
and leave the kid with a stiff on her hands.

I stopped along the way and called a homicide cop I know at
LAPD, reported the shooting. Told him I'd done it, told him who
the guy was, and as much of the circumstances as I felt ready to
divulge. Of course he immediately wanted me to come in and
make a full statement and I immediately told him to go to hell.
"Just put it in the record that I called it in," I requested. "I'm not
coming in until I get the thing unraveled."

I hung up while he was still trying to argue me in; for all I
knew, someone had been expecting me to call and was already
tracing it. In these days of computerized switching, a trace can
be fearfully swift if you are already set up to run it. And, see, I
was already totally paranoid.

I made another stop, at an all-night supermarket in the East
Valley for vital groceries, then took my charge straight from
there to the hideout. Place belongs to a friend who now lives in
Mexico, it's away up in the boonies in San Bernardino County
about 75 minutes from the L.A. Civic Center, and I've had a key
for a long time. Good spot for fishing and philosophizing, sits on

the bank of a little mountain stream that runs strong and steady during the snow and melt, reduces to a step-across trickle during the summer but is always pretty and even fishable at trickle state.

It was nearing onto four o'clock when we got up there, and my frightened nymphet had calmed enough to fall asleep on my shoulder. She'd been curled up there for at least twenty minutes and awoke with a disoriented start when I killed the engine. Guess it isn't proper to refer to her as a "nymphet" although she sure looked like one, especially sleeping. See, I'm six-three and weighed two-sixty last time I looked. I'm just a bit on the down side of forty, too, and though I make this "kid" at twenty-eight at a minimum, considering her history, she has the slender undeveloped look of an undersized teenager—and the face doesn't help you that much, either, because it looks an old-soul fourteen. You know what I mean—that sweet-sober look of super intelligence that some kids have and never lose no matter how old they get. This one looked very frail and vulnerable on top of it, but I was to discover the illusion of that before the night was over.

The place is built sort of like a ski chalet, you know, all woodsy and fireplacey, very snug and comfortable but not a hell of a lot of room. Two rooms, in fact, one up and one down—and the one "up" is merely an open loft that sleeps ten communally, twenty if the mood is right and the inhibitions are down. I guess that loft has seen a few twenty-somes in its time but never with me. I'd been invited to a few of those group-gropes but guess my inhibitions were never that far down. Come to think of it, maybe I am more the old-fashioned kind of guy. Not shy—not when it's one on one, guy and gal, right time and place—no, I'm not shy but I am a bit choosey.

I would not have chosen the nymphet.

Not that she wasn't appealing as hell and all that, she was just not the kind to usually get my juices stirring and I wasn't even thinking along those lines when I took her there. I mean, this was community service on my part...period.

She loved the place.

I carried the groceries in and built a fire while she wandered around and explored the facilities. The "down" room was an all-in-one living room, dining room, kitchen, game alcove, bar—all of it dominated by a massive fireplace that covered an entire outside wall. Had the usual couches and chairs, tables and all the gracious trimmings, big furry rug across the hearth. The kitchen was modern and well-equipped with all the amenities, so was the bathroom, so was all of it. This was designed as a party pad, see. The "game alcove" featured a Jacuzzi and sauna, had a compact fold-down ping-pong table for when you weren't spa-ing, a shelf loaded with board games and other quiet diversions.

No television.

My friend hated television. The opiate of the masses, she called it, paraphrasing Karl Marx. My friend loved to party, but now she was doing it all in Mexico and this place was mine any time I needed it.

So now I needed it and I figured we might as well get comfortable.

I put on coffee for me, hot water for tea for the nymphet, and she went delightedly to the shower. The fire was leaping and crackling, warming the chill night air and lighting the room with a rosy glow when she came out of there.

She came out stark naked, I swear.

And I immediately had to revise my assessment of her womanly charms. Funny, isn't it, how clothing can so confuse the eye. What looked frail and girlish in skirt and blouse had bloomed out entirely womanly in the naked truth, perfectly proportioned and downright voluptuous with perfectly sculpted breasts and softly flowing lines in total harmony all the way.

She walked past me as though I were not there and went to the kitchen to make her tea, brought it back to the hearth and knelt there on one knee to gaze into the flames while she sipped the tea—turned once to give me a sweet smile as though saying "thanks"—and I was damn near thunderstruck through all of it, I mean this was a rare vision of absolute beauty—you know, the dance of flames in the fireplace, that glowing skin reflecting the firelight—that pose, damn, that pose, like something you would see on display at the Louvre as a masterwork, and it just simply wiped me out.

Presently I got up and poured my coffee, took it with me to the bathroom, sipped it as I shaved and showered and wondered.

Wondered, yeah.

It came as a surprise to realize that I wasn't scared anymore, I was breathing all the way without pain or stricture, and the raw scratches along the whole length of my body were not smarting under the soapy scrubdown.

She was still there beside the fire just as I had left her when I came out, the same way she'd come out. She looked at me with a smile, that same sweet "thank you" smile, and spoke her first words in the naked truth. "Does your body hurt?"

"Not anymore," I told her. "How 'bout yours?"

I guess she'd refilled her teacup. I could see the steam rising from it as she delicately sipped the brew. "I will massage it if you would like."

"Sounds nice," I said, and went to both knees at the other side of the fireplace.

"When I was a little girl..."

"Yeah?"

"I would awaken sometimes in the night, frightened. My father would come into my bedroom and lie down beside me. He would touch me lovingly and rub my tummy until I was no longer frightened."

"Sounds like dangerous stuff to me," I told her.

"Yes, and so my mother felt. It is why she divorced my father. But I have missed my father ever since."

"Especially when you wake up frightened."

"Yes. And there is no one to rub my tummy."

She set the teacup down and stretched out on her back in front of the fire, that beautiful head touching my knees, looking up at me with those Siamese eyes. They had gone sort of smoky, mysterious, inviting.

"I'm not your father, kid," I warned her.

"Believe me you are not," she warned me back.

So what the hell, I rubbed her belly. To tell the naked truth, I rubbed every delightful thing she had.

CHAPTER

FIVE

SPECTACULAR SEX is the quickest and nicest way to forge an intimate bond between a man and a woman. I'm sure that most women mean well and think they're onto something very important when they delay sex with a guy until they think they know him well, but there's something paradoxical about the idea. First, you are never going to know each other well enough until you've shared each other in sex, that's basic to the male-female mystery; and, secondly, the very process of getting closely acquainted often sets up little deceits and dishonesties that eventually get in the way of good sex.

On the other hand—listen up, ladies—the quickest way to a man's honest feelings, to really open him up, is to fuck his brains out. Sounds simplistic and crude, I know, but it's true. What you get then is the raw man, as he really is. If that's what

39

you're after. Need to be honest with yourself too, of course. Do you really want to get to know the guy?—or do you just want to know how amenable he may be to a long-term commitment? See, there has always been something basically dishonest—you know, like cold and calculating—in that approach too. I mean if you're dangling the possibility of sex in front of a guy's aroused masculinity while really you are going for the rest of his life... see, that's a con right there and the guy knows it. So he cons you back, and maybe you deserved it. But if you both go into it for the magical moment that is there, then you both get that moment—and the rest is going to play out the same in either approach anyway, and meanwhile you've cut through all the fancy footwork of bait and trap. You have to be sensible about it, of course. Don't start with an obvious sleazebag, but you don't want to start there in any case—so if you start with a nice guy, why inject your own soft brand of sleaze into it?

I'm not trying to sound like Doctor Ruth, don't get me wrong, but I've had a lot of experience with the male-female mystery and also I have given it a lot of thought lately. Nothing turns me off faster anymore than to have a new lady trying to get into my head while I'm trying to get her into my bed. I don't believe in casual sex either, but maybe you and I don't mean the same thing by that. See, if you're focussing on my head instead of my glands then you're having casual sex with me. I believe in commitment too—commitment to the act, and total focus on the emotional states of loving.

If you are wondering how committed I may become to your general care and feeding, then you're focussing on the future instead of the now—and good sex, my dear, is always in the now.

It certainly was that night with Gina. Maybe we were partially set up for it by the shared experience of danger and anxiety, but I think primarily it was simply the fact that a man and woman with no expectations of each other and a very brief shared history came together in a spontaneous burst of electricity and there was nothing between us to serve as insulation.

It certainly was spectacular, and it certainly did open us to each other in a way that probably would never have occurred otherwise. We lay in front of the fire and talked until dawn. She told me things that she'd probably never told another man. I know damn well I told her things that I'd never told a woman. We got to know each other in the way that counts, and in a way that I guess we could never take back if we wanted to.

Don't get me wrong. I couldn't have written this lady's biography from what I learned about her that morning. That's not the kind of "knowing" I'm talking about. I couldn't tell you what she liked for dinner, or what she liked in a man, certainly not how she might react to this situation or that. But I felt very close to this woman and I would have defended her life with my own, without stint or hesitation. That's the kind of knowing that counts. It's nonverbal and indescribable, but it is the kind of knowing that makes true friendship possible in a dog-eat-dog world.

Problem was, I still did not know whether she was friend or foe. At the moment, I did not particularly care.

But I guess I should have given it some thought.

We fell asleep by the fire as the sun was rising and she was gone when I woke up several hours later. Gone, yeah, split— stolen away like a thief. Take that literally, because gone also was the little packet of stuff I'd filched from the consulate. Also my gun, the S&W I'd been packing around all those years—a very sentimental loss.

As bad as anything else, I was marooned up there with no telephone, no neighbors, no wheels, and only my feet for deliverance.

About the only consolation I could find was that I was still alive. I was mad as hell, sure, but mostly at myself. If she'd conned me then at least she'd done it honestly. I mean, those hours we'd had together beside the fireplace had been genuine.

I had some eggs for fortification—it was a five-mile walk to the crossroad, the nearest civilized point—then I tidied the place up, locked it up, and started my trek.

You can do a lot of thinking on a five-mile walk. I thought of many things but came to no specific conclusions about anything. I could only hope that Gina was straight, that Tom was straight, and that she was genuinely committed to helping him through the mess. Didn't know where that left me, of course, but I had already decided to hang it up. While we lay there talking in front of the fire I knew that I was in a foolish game and that I needed to get out of it. So I'd already made the decision, before I fell asleep that morning, that I was going in. I would return Tom's five-grand retainer and turn everything else over to the cops, let them sort it out—and if I had to cool my heels in jail for a while, well okay, I could live through that too. But I did not want to play this cloak-and-dagger game.

I didn't mention this to Gina, of course, but maybe some of it was communicated to her nonverbally. Maybe she sensed my lagging spirit in the matter and decided to preempt me.

She would do that, yeah.

On the other hand, if she were not straight...

Well, see, I had reason enough to wonder about that, too, but not for very long. I didn't quite make it down to the junction, not on foot. This car came along, headed the other way, and stopped for me. A Mercedes with tinted windows, couldn't see into it very well and didn't need to because a rear door opened and this guy got out.

It was Ivan the Terrible.

I said, "Hi", and he said nothing, just stood there with a gun on me until I voluntarily surrendered my only remaining armament, the little stun gun, then my new pals the Russkies gave me a lift back into town.

THESE GUYS were no great conversationalists. Maybe they spoke no English but they didn't speak much of anything else to each other either. I was in front with the driver and another guy kept Ivan company in the back. Ivan would not have fit into that front seat, I'm not kidding, and he did not put his gun away the whole time. Every time I moved in the seat he waggled it at me as though to remind me that it was there, but hell I needed no reminders.

Funny thing happened on the way to the consulate, however.

We were moving sedately along the Santa Monica Freeway just east of the East L.A. interchange when a motorcycle CHP pulled us over. The driver looked mad as hell about that—we'd been cruising at 55 on the button all the way. He brought the big car to a smooth halt on the shoulder, grabbed his papers and jumped out to meet the cop at the rear. I had just a glimpse of him pointing to his license plate and had a mental image of what that might look like, in terms of diplomatic immunity, before another car pulled in behind the motorcycle and two guys jumped out.

They had FBI written all over them, and I didn't know whether to be glad or sad.

I could see resignation in big Ivan's eyes as he put his gun away, and it could not have been a better cue.

"Thanks for the lift," I said to the back seat, and got the hell out of there.

The feds hustled me into their car and the Mercedes was still sitting there when we pulled away. It had been a damned quick switch, enough to make a guy dizzy, but I really did not know whether I had moved from the frying pan or the fire. There were three of these guys too—I was sandwiched between two of them in the back seat—and they were hardly more communicative than the others had been.

"Tell you why I called..." I said weakly as we sped off onto the interchange, hoping I guess that a little humor couldn't hurt a thing.

"Shut up," the one to my right said softly.

"Mighty Joe Copp," sneered the other.

Those were the final words for both of them, literally.

Yet another car pulled abreast to our left and I saw before I heard what it meant. The snout of an automatic weapon was showing in the open rear window. Either I saw quicker or my reflexes were better but I reacted before the others, turned to liquid damn quick and slid toward the floor just as that chatter-gun opened up and swept our car from stern to stem and back to stern again. The guys beside me were spouting blood at the first cough and I guess the driver too because we were airborne off that ramp and hurtling through thin air while I was still trying to get down all the way.

We came down hard, very hard—squarely on the nose, I think, and kept on bouncing along for what seemed an eternity. The silence that descended after the final bounce and quiver was like the final sigh as the world is dying. It came as something of a surprise to discover that I myself was not dead or even dying. I was lying halfway out of the wreckage on my back and all the pieces of me seemed to be present and accounted for. I tested them all first then slithered on clear. I was in grass and I could see a freeway ramp above me. I could smell raw gasoline, too, and that helped propel me along the grass until I could find my feet and get them under me. I was dizzy and queasy but appropriately thankful to be feeling anything at all.

The freeway ramp was about thirty feet above my head and other motorists apparently were stopping up there and going to the shattered rail for a look-see. I didn't need or want any of that either. I kept moving, not knowing or caring where so long as it was away from the scene. Not far away I could see the upper floors of L.A. County Hospital and that sort of oriented me as to place, and at least it was a comforting passing thought that I was close to medical help if I needed it.

But that was not the kind of help I needed.

What I needed, pal, nobody alive could provide.

CHAPTER
SIX

THE IDEA was coming home to me that someone was trying to make me dead but I really couldn't understand why, not at that point. Okay, granted that the guys at the consulate could have reason to be a little upset at me, that should not translate as a motive for murdr unless I was into something a lot heavier than I realized—and anyway, if that had been their game—to make me dead—they could have done it much easier on that deserted mountain road where they'd picked me up. Why haul me all the way back into L.A. just to kill me?

But that was only one of the questions tugging at my dazed mind at the moment. Obviously the motorcycle cop had stopped that car with the diplomatic plates not for any traffic infraction but only to spring me out of it. How had anyone even known that I was in that car? I had long since accepted the unhappy conclusion that Gina had turned me to the Russkies, which explained how they found me, but how could the feds have known about that unless they had been watching the whole thing?—and if they had been watching, why did they wait until we were all the way back into L.A. before moving on it? Again, the intercept would have been much easier and cleaner in the boonies, so why wait? Another: if they were that intent on capturing the killer of one of their own, why the soft collar?—why didn't they close in force and have the whole damned area nailed down the way they usually do?—why do it with a single CHP on motorcycle and no backup whatever? Finally: why the daring hit on FBI agents in broad daylight on a busy freeway, and who was responsible for that?

None of it made much sense, not with myself in the crosshairs. Why all that desperate attention on a small-time private cop who didn't even understand the attention?

Strange, isn't it, how some insignificant item of information can be presented to the mind during a peak moment when the mind is focussed on other things, so the item buries itself in some obscure cell of the brain where it could lie forever unnoticed—but then another peak moment brings it howling out of there and it bangs you squarely between the eyes. In my latest telephone conversation with Tom Chase he had given me precise instructions on what to look for and where to find it in Gudgaloff's office. "It's a black book about the size of a passport, soft leather cover, about fifty pages of vellum quality paper, keeps it in the upper left drawer of his desk." I had wondered at the time how Tom knew all that, but then I figured my question was answered when Gina mentioned "Nicky's black book" in a way that made me think she'd had some kind of personal relationship with the Russian.

I leafed quickly through the book when I found it, just to verify that it was the right one—and of course my mind was busy on several other fronts at the same moment. All I saw in that quick scan was what I expected to see—cryptic jottings in a language I don't savvy but here and there an obvious name. One of the names that leapt into that quick scan was *Cherche,* and it leapt at me only because it is an odd name that I had encountered before and in a strangely similar context: the Russian language.

Years ago when I was with the San Francisco police I knew a gal who called herself Cherche LaFemme. Sounds like a stage name, doesn't it—and it is, but not in the usual sense. Cherche had a stable of high-priced call girls and I think she probably did tricks herself now and then. I think she borrowed her name from the French phrase "cherchez la femme" but Cherche (pronounced *Sher-she*) was from San Francisco's aristocratic Russian community. Very flamboyant lady and known to all the vice cops but we pretty much left her alone because she ran such a clean operation and, besides, she had political clout.

Cherche stuck in my mind all the more because I ran into her again just a couple of years ago right here in Los Angeles. She'd grown even prettier with age, like the Gabor girls, and claimed to be retired but I'd figured at the time that this old whore would die a whore and I think I was right. She was running some kind of high-class operation out of Beverly Hills, I was sure of that, but it wasn't any of my business anymore so I didn't look into it.

As I was saying, I saw the name in Gudgaloff's book but it didn't register until I was hoofing it along the back streets following that freeway shooting and trying to put the puzzle together in my mind. Even then it didn't come with any clarity but it sizzled just the same and I knew that somewhere down deep my mind had made a connection that ought to figure into the problem. Maybe it was just a straw but I was ready to grab at anything, so I put Cherche on a front burner as necessary business to be looked into as soon as the elements of mere survival had been attended to.

As for that, obviously I needed to rethink my decision to withdraw from the case, primarily because it was beginning to appear that I would not survive a withdrawal. Apparently someone thought I knew more than I knew I knew, and that someone was willing to take drastic action to prevent me from telling anyone else what I didn't know I knew. And of course if there were kinky feds involved—as Tom had suspected—then I was now in the same boat that he was in, whatever that was, and we both probably would hang if we should live so long.

No, I couldn't go in.

Not yet, anyway.

I had to get some answers first, and I had to find a place to begin looking for those answers.

I guess that is why Cherche came banging back from my gray matter. The larger mind was trying to tell me: start here.

So okay, I would do that.

But first I had to get organized. I had to get some arms. And I had to get some wheels. Then I could try getting my head on straight.

A MEXICAN kid was sipping a coke in a sharply customized low-rider pickup truck outside a hamburger stand near the hospital. I showed him fifty bucks and told him, "I'll give you this to take me home. It's less than an hour from here."

He looked me up and down, not liking what he saw and with

plenty good reason. I looked a mess. "Who kicked the shit out of you, man?"

"Nobody you'd know," I said. "They took my car. I gotta get home. How 'bout it?"

He looked at the money and then again at me, up and down. "I don't want you riding inside my cab, man. You'll get it all dirty."

I threw in another ten and told him, "I'll ride in back. Go north on Mission, for starters."

"How far we going, man?"

"Sixty bucks worth," I told him. "Where else can you earn it in an hour?"

He took the money without a smile, I climbed into the bed, and we headed out Mission Road. That would link up with Huntington through South Pasadena and San Marino, get me up into the foothills, then we'd work our way eastward while avoiding the freeways. So maybe it would take a little more than an hour on surface streets. It was still the best offer this kid would get all week—and I would break his surly face if he tried anything shitty on me.

He didn't, and he drove the pickup like there were eggs inside the tires and he didn't want to break any, so it took an hour and a half to get into my neck of the hills. I gave the kid a twenty-dollar bonus and got out a half-mile shy, hoofed it the rest of the way in a cautious approach, slipped in through the rear.

Didn't know if the house was under surveillance, didn't know if a posse of feds were camped inside, but I had to chance it because I had nowhere else to regroup and get it together. Besides which, I was aching to be home for a while, to find some comfort. It had been a hell of a day already and I knew that it was going to get worse before it got better.

I hurt everywhere. Literally. Even my hairs hurt. I was torn and bloodied, scratched and bruised, looked like a wino two weeks in the gutter and felt like the walking dead, and I was damned glad to see my castle. At the moment, I think I would have fought for possession of it. But I didn't have to. I live in a somewhat isolated area on a mountainside overlooking the San Gabriel Valley, in a neighborhood of "horse estates" where folks value their seclusion and privacy. I have acreage, lots of shrubbery and trees, and neighbors who mind their own.

Someone wanting to stake out my house would probably set up at the entrance to a little lane that serves my place and several others, and from that point they could not even see my place but they could monitor all movements in and out by vehicle. My only fear was that someone could be waiting for me inside the house.

But all seemed well in there. I entered through a patio door into my study which is also my bedroom and office, stealthily checked the whole place out room by room before I took an easy breath. Then the first thing I did was put on the coffeepot. The second thing I did was turn on the heater for the Jacuzzi, which also is part of my study-bedroom-office, and the third thing, was to strip naked and throw the clothing I'd been wearing into the trash.

Then I went to the gun cabinet and broke out the arsenal, selected a riot gun and a couple of revolvers, rounded up ammo and took the whole bundle into my study to make it all ready for war. The coffee was hot by the time I was finished with that. I took some frozen pastries from the freezer and heated them in the microwave, took the whole thing into the Jacuzzi with me and made like a hedonist for about thirty minutes.

Felt almost human again after that. Almost. For a moment. Then I checked my telephone answering machine. Had eight messages. Three were personal, one was someone trying to sell me a legal plan, two were on routine business matters I'd been working on, one was from the homicide cop I'd called the night before, and one was from old pal Tom Chase.

The friend from homicide wanted me to call him the minute I came in. Sure. The call had been received at 12:17 P.M. Way I calculate it, that was about twenty minutes after someone shot me off a freeway.

The call from Tom Chase had been recorded the day before. It was timed in at 3:45 P.M., about half an hour after I'd departed for the consulate, and he'd been in a hell of a sweat.

"Don't go," was the message. "I'm calling it off. I'm sending someone to intercept you in case you don't get this message in time. If you do get the message, don't call me back and in fact don't attempt any contact whatever. I'll get back to you when I can. And Joe... good luck."

Good luck, sure.

I played the message three times while I rummaged for a stashed, trying-to-quit cigarette—never did find it—while darkly ruminating over that "good luck" wish to someone who'd just been fired from a dangerous mission. That should have been good luck enough in itself, so why...?

Why had he tried to cancel it, when obviously he was still in a hell of a sweat?

What was he sweating over?—and what was he trying to warn me about in that "good luck" goodbye?

I was sitting there naked and troubled, trying to put it together, when I heard a noise from somewhere in the front of the house. I didn't go for a cover-up, just scooped up one of the revolvers and went to check it out.

I surprised Gina Terrabona in the entry hall, and she surprised the hell out of me too.

She was holding my big blunderbuss in one hand and a burglar tool in the other.

I said, "Thanks for bringing the gun back. Just drop it right there, that'll be fine."

She said, "So you *are* alive," but she did not drop the gun.

"No thanks to you," I replied. She was half a pound of trigger-pull short of dead herself, but I guess I wasn't fully committed to that yet.

"I am glad nevertheless," she said as she backed warily through the open doorway. She pulled the door closed behind her and I just stood there like a ninny and let her do it.

A few hours earlier I would have died for the lady.

Guess I just wasn't ready yet to fully reverse that idea. So maybe, indeed, I would die for her yet.

CHAPTER

SEVEN

MY SECOND set of wheels is a van I use for special work such as extended surveillance and photo assignments, keep it in my garage at home most of the time because I really love the old Cad and enjoy driving it even though it guzzles gas at about twice the rate as the van. Fuel economy was not the reason I bought the van anyway. It can be very useful to a guy in my line of work. I had an assortment of magnetic decals to dress it up to fit the job. It was currently wearing identification as *Consolidated Cable Services* and that was good enough, all I wanted at the moment was transportation. I put the riot gun in a clip behind the seat and loaded in several other comfort items then got away from there as quickly as I could, didn't exactly feel like entertaining any more visitors.

My curiosity regarding a stake-out was satisfied when I

reached the main road. A car was parked in the bushes just above the junction with my lane, two men in the front seat and they were giving me an interested look as I stopped for the intersection. So let them look. I was dressed for the van, in utility jacket and a Dodgers cap, hornrimmed clear-glass spectacles and stick-on sideburns to the bottom of my jaw—best friends would not have recognized me right off. Besides, these guys were looking for incoming traffic and apparently with a single purpose. They'd allowed Gina access and departure, obviously, so...

So what the hell, I figured I'd better cover the bases. I turned right, uphill, instead of my usual left, downhill, and stopped directly across from them, rolled down my window and yelled over, "What?—are you guys in trouble?"

The one in the driver's seat called back, "Just checking our map. That's a dead-end road you just came out of, isn't it? You been in there all day?"

These guys were not local cops, maybe not any kind of cops. Maybe feds, maybe anything, but the guy definitely had East Coast in his voice.

I told him, "Naw, I just came through. What're you looking for?"

That hit him hard. "What do you mean, you came through? It shows dead-end."

I said, "You must have an old map," and I eased on up the hill.

Part of me hated to do it to the guys, the part that has empathy for long, boring vigils, but most of me served them right. Last I saw through my rearview was one of them sprinting across the roadway and headed down the lane for a quick check on foot. It would take him at least five minutes to get back to the car. By then I would be well clear of the area and rolling free. Or so I figured, anyway.

I T WAS seven o'clock and getting dark when I reached the
other side of Los Angeles and rolled into Beverly Hills. It's a
cold city, if you know what I mean, a wallet for a heart, and
you feel it immediately. Merely to get your mail there is regarded as an item of prestige and many people who do that do
not live or work there. So maybe it's a business or career advantage for some people—but if it is, what does that say about the
rest of us?

Whatever, it's a cold city and I don't know why anyone would
live there. Well, okay, maybe I did know why Cherche LaFemme
would want to live there. When I call this lady a whore, please
understand that this is on the same order as referring to Queen
Elizabeth as a government employee. When it comes to classify-
ing people by occupation, there are grades and levels that should
be considered if you want a clear picture.

Cherche paid five times what it was worth to live in Beverly
Hills for the same reason that most other people do: it helped
her image in a town where image is everything.

It is also obviously a town under siege. Down in the ordinary
Los Angeles neighborhoods where the common people live you
see houses with bars on doors and windows and you understand
why they are there, to keep the crime outside. Beverly Hills
doesn't have bars for the most part but it has walls and private
security outfits that patrol constantly and every house has a sign
stuck in the yard to warn of Maginot Line electronic defenses to
keep the crime outside. Talk about East Berlin and the paranoia
of the Berlin Wall, the Hills of Beverly have become a virtual war
zone where nobody walks the streets day or night or even shows
themselves in the open air, and no one seems to know or care

that they've locked themselves in as securely as they've locked the world out—so what is a prison or internment camp, anyway, and what price is too high for prestige?

But I can understand it, I guess. Especially for people like Cherche. She was born to a financially diminished but proud family who'd been undone by the Bolshevik revolution more than a quarter of a century before her birth, fleeing with their lives and little else to an uncertain future in America, but she'd been raised in the aristocratic tradition and taught that common work was beneath her, schooled in the arts but not in any practical way, and she'd emerged into young womanhood with aged parents and totally unrealistic expectations of the modern world.

But she had uncommon beauty and she could move with ease in the highest social circles, and she discovered quickly that men of wealth and power would protect her if given reason to do so.

What else was a girl to do?

She gave them reason.

But she was not a total airhead, either, knowing that both youth and beauty were fleeting, so she set out early to carve a lasting niche for herself in the financial fabric of this country. When I first came across her in San Francisco, she was about twenty-eight years old but already firmly established in the fabric of that city. I remember that I had been surprised to discover many years later that she had relocated to Southern California, so well entrenched and protected had she been up north. It's two entirely different worlds, you know, San Francisco and L.A.—different kinds of folks, different kinds of strokes, and seldom do the two come together in any accommodation or agreement.

But, as I said, I'd been busy with other things when I found Cherche in L.A. We had briefly renewed our entirely casual friendship then gone our separate ways, and I guess I'd never have thought of her again but for a cryptic note in a mysterious book viewed briefly in the dead of the night at the Russians' new consulate in L.A.

I could undertand Cherche in Beverly Hills, yeah. She could feel right at home there. It was a cold city, sure, but a natural environment for anyone in Cherche's business because any guy living there was willing to pay five times what anything was worth.

She had one of the older places closer in, just north of Santa Monica and east of Rodeo, on a palm-lined street and behind five-foot walls. Had to announce myself at the gate to get an electronic unlock so she knew I was there and had plenty of time to prepare herself but just the same I found her in a slinky negligee and bedroom slippers—and, yeah, she still had it, all of it, a very beautiful woman who'd made a business all her life out of being beautiful.

As usual, too, she was attended by beautiful younger women—undaunted by that kind of competition and always mindful of the importance of catering to male fantasy. One was her secretary, she said, and the other obviously a maid, but you wouldn't know for sure which was which by the difference in attire and you found your eyes always drawn back to Cherche anyway.

I knew she had to be close to fifty but who gave a damn when the woman looked like this woman, sounded like this woman, moved like this woman. We'd never gotten it on, in case you're wondering, but not from any squeamishness on my part. I never held whoring against a woman if it was done artfully, and I'd as soon lie with one of those as any other where true love is not involved. The flirtation had always been there but time, place and circumstance had just not converged for the two of us so it had never gone beyond that.

She made me comfortable and plied me with cognac but kept the other two nearby as we talked old times in her "game room." I don't know what kind of games she usually played there but it was loaded with expensive couches and chairs, had a small dance floor and bar, pool table, several electronic arcade-style games.

Presently there was no way to avoid the reason for my visit so I told her straight out: "Your name came up in a current investigation. I was wondering if you know Nicholas Gudgaloff."

She pursed lips that can pout so prettily, looked me straight in the eye and replied, "Of course I know Nicky. We are cousins, darling. Well... kissing cousins, I hope—second or third, maybe. Why do you ask?"

Well of course I was a little bowled over. Cherche had never expressed anything better than utter contempt for anything communist and it had always been my impression that she was a couple of steps to the right of Ronald Reagan when it came to American politics. So I said to her, "That must be a bit awkward for you. Gudgaloff is the KGB boss for this district."

Cherche found the statement quite amusing. "Don't be ridiculous, darling. Nicky is the perfect gentleman, descended directly from Catherine the Great's branch of the family. He is the new trade attaché in Los Angeles, and it is a perfect stroke for *perestroika,* the new capitalist movement in Russia."

"Capitalist movement, eh?"

"Well we knew they would have to realize the error sooner or later, didn't we? But heavens, who would have thought it would have taken them this long? KGB!—really, Joseph, this is too funny, my darling. I cannot wait to tell Nicky about this."

"Do you see him often?"

"Oh, well, often enough, I suppose. One has duties. We manage."

I asked her, "Are you working with him on this *perestroika* stuff?"

"One does what one can, darling. Is it not time now to encourage Mother Russia to rejoin the community of civilized nations?"

"How do you do that, Cherche?"

"Do what, darling?"

"How do you encourage...? Uh, what do you do for Nicky?"

She gave me an impish smile and replied, "One does what one does best."

"I see," I said.

"You do?" She was teasing me.

I was grinning as I replied, "One cannot look the other way all the time, can one?"

"Always the policeman," she said.

"Do you know Tom Chase?"

"Oh yes, charming man and quite handsome too. But how do you know him, Joseph?"

"We were cops together," I said. "Here in L.A., before I went private."

Guess I'd said the wrong thing, from her point of view—the right thing, from my own. Cherche was aghast at that information. "But when was this?"

"Just a few years ago."

"That is quite impossible, Joseph!"

I spread my hands and gave her the knowing look. "Would I lie to you, Cherche?"

She turned immediately to the secretary and commanded, "Bring Angélique!"

The secretary went softly away. Cherche agitatedly offered me a long cigarette which I thought about very strongly before declining. She lit one and settled back onto her couch, keeping her eyes averted.

The girl came in behind me and stood in the doorway to ask, "You sent for me, Cherche?"

I didn't even have to look around. I knew the voice. And I knew "Angélique." I would have died for her earlier that day.

CHAPTER
EIGHT

I WILL have to say, she handled it very well. Better than I did, maybe. She gave me only a cursory glance as she came on into the room, showing no reaction other than a clenching of one tiny fist. Cherche introduced her as Angélique and me as Joseph, offered her a drink which was declined, offered to top mine off and I accepted, then she got right down to it.

"My dear, such a delightfully small world, Joseph is a friend of your Mr. Chase."

"Which is to say that he was referred by him," Gina replied, without a look my way.

"Oh no." Cherche laughed softly, took a sip of cognac and a swipe at the cigarette. "Joseph is an old friend of mine also. But there seems to be some confusion about...he says your Mr. Chase has lived in Los Angeles for many years."

I got a veiled look from that one, just a quick sweep of the eyes—a bit defiant, a bit pleading. "Then obviously it could not be the same Mr. Chase."

Cherche explained to me, "Angélique's Tom Chase is a businessman from Tel Aviv."

I grinned and replied, "So what's in a name? I haven't seen Tom for years. But I saw the name on a report and figured it was the same guy." I looked directly at Gina, nearly caught her eye. "I was hoping it was. But it's not a small world, after all."

Cherche was not ready to let it go at that. "What does your Tom Chase look like, Joseph?"

I said, "No, I figured it was the wrong guy when you called him charming and handsome. That's not mine. Mine's a cop, ugly and mean."

That seemed to settle the matter to Cherche's satisfaction.

Couldn't tell how Gina took it. There was nothing in the eyes or voice to clue the feelings as she said to Cherche, "It is a common name in America, no? Like Chase Manhattan bank."

Cherche winked at me as she replied to Gina, "Bring that one over too, my dear, if you should meet."

Gina smiled and immediately withdrew, recognizing the dismissal in Cherche's voice. As soon as she was out of earshot, I asked, "Who is Angélique?"

"The daughter of an old friend," Cherche explained. "She is new in this country, from Israel. Do you like her?"

I ignored the question. "Mind telling me who that old friend is?"

"Why should I, darling?"

I said, "Okay, you mind. Did the guy come with her?"

"Which guy?"

"Tom Chase."

"Why do you ask?"

"Why do you care if I ask, Cherche?"

She put out her cigarette, made a small face at me. "Always the policeman, Joseph. You make me nervous sometimes. Please don't."

"I am not a policeman anymore."

"Ah, but I think you are. You are playing mind games with me, are you not? All this business with Tom Chase!—were you merely angling for an introduction to Angélique?" She laughed suddenly, set down her cognac to shake a playful finger at me. "Nicky, ah?—the KGB? Come now, Joseph. What do you want from me?"

I grinned back at her, reminded her, "We go back a long way, Cherche. Have I ever been anything but a friend?"

"Ah, but..."

"But?"

She studied me for a moment then relaxed back onto the soft couch with a smile. "Very well. How can I help you, darling?"

"Just give me straight answers to a few simple questions."

"If they are simple, fair enough. Ask. But hurry. My business is night business and it does not await my pleasure."

"Are you still in business?"

"Yes."

"Is Angélique one of your girls?"

"Yes and no. Do you like her? I must warn that you perhaps cannot afford Angélique."

"Maybe you can't either. Are you supplying girls for Nicky?"

"From time to time, yes. Oh, but not for his personal use, you understand. What did you mean, I cannot afford...?"

"Just kidding. How long has Angélique been with you?"

"A few months. Why are you so—?"

"Have you sent her on appointments for Nicky?"

"I will not answer that."

"How does Tom Chase figure into anything?"

She stared at me blankly for a moment before replying, "Business arrangements."

"What kind of business arrangements? *Perestroika?*"

"I think so, yes."

"So Chase has been doing business with Nicky?"

"This I do not know."

"But you said *perestroika,* yes. So..."

"As an intermediary, perhaps."

"Involving Israel?"

She daintily shrugged her shoulders. "He is from Israel, so perhaps. Perhaps not. Israelis are not always interested only in Israel. Business is business, Joseph, you must know. None of this is my concern. My business is entertainment, and this is all I know, but also my business is discretion. Already I have been entirely too indiscreet in matters involving clients, so please do not keep on with this."

I got to my feet, said, "Okay. I can respect that. Just satisfy my curiosity about something. How did you and Nicky happen to get together? How long has he been in this country?"

"He came with the new trade delegation last year," she replied.

"He looked you up?"

"To be sure, with greetings and messages from long lost relatives."

"He wasn't looking for Cherche LaFemme, was he," I said teasingly.

"In a way, yes, it seems he was," she teased me back.

The French phrase she borrowed for her professional name means "look for the woman."

It seemed to fit this case very well.

But which woman?

IT HAD occurred to me at some point during that tense confrontation with Gina Terrabona that all I knew about the lady was what she herself had told me. So, hell, I knew nothing at all about her, for sure—didn't know her real name, for sure —didn't know her real background, for sure—didn't know for sure if she'd given me a single word of truth. Her name could be Gina or Angélique or Molly or whatever. I didn't know what her real connection was with Tom Chase, or if she worked for PowerTron or had ever seen the Pentagon or Israel. The whole thing could be a fabric of lies.

Something else clicked at me during that moment of questions, too.

Tom had tried to call off the consulate job, even said he was sending someone to intercept me in case I missed his message. Gina, on the other hand, had told me that Tom had been preparing to back me up outside the consulate when he was arrested —and though she knew he'd been arrested, she'd said nothing about his attempt to cancel the burglary. But wait a minute...!

How did I even know that Tom had been arrested?

I knew it only because Gina had told me that.

So, dammit... how could I even believe that?

Another thing... how did I know that Gina had gone down there to back me up? My first impression of the intervention was that someone was trying to run me down with a car. What if I'd been right about that, and what if that someone had simply run out of nerve when I planted and challenged, opted for a softer game?

See, all of that was boiling through my head and I was feeling sort of sick about it all when I said goodbye to Cherche and let myself out. Night had fully fallen and no lights were helping relieve the darkness outside, so I was groping half-blind toward my car on unfamiliar turf when a soft hand grabbed mine.

It was Gina, she had my S&W and she was handing it over. "Thank you for the loan," she said quietly. "And thank you for not blowing my cover in there. Now I must go quickly before I am discovered."

I said, "Wait, wait..."

"There's no time. Tom got a message to me. He says you should go for Putnam and Delancey. They—"

"Who?"

"Morris Putnam and George Delancey, PowerTron executives. He says they are the key."

"What did you do with the stuff from Gudgaloff's office?"

"I put it into the proper hands. Please, Joe..." She stretched up and planted a moist kiss on my lips then danced away and disappeared into the shadows beside the house.

I stood there for as moment wanting a cigarette in the worst way. "Bullshit," I said out loud to the quiet Beverly Hills night, then went on to the car.

It was all bullshit, sure.

But it was all I had to work with. I would do that, sure, for a while. I just did not want to die for it.

I especially did not want to die for a woman who did not deserve it. But I was hooked, yeah. I was hooked on Gina-Angélique-whoever even standing neck deep in total bullshit.

And I guess that scared me most of all.

CHAPTER
NINE

GINA HAD returned an empty gun. I wondered if she had been afraid to hand me a loaded one or if she just hadn't liked carrying it around that way. There had been no mention of my abandonment in the mountains or her later forced entry into my home when obviously she'd thought me dead, no hint of apology, no attempt to explain anything. Nevertheless I went away feeling a bit better about the whole thing. She had kissed me, after all, and she seemed to be assuming that we were still playing on the same team.

So I felt a little better about it all, yeah, but not for long because I picked up a tail right outside the joint and I couldn't shake it after four turns and a run along Santa Monica in heavy traffic. Never got close enough for any kind of identification but just hung back there very expertly and went everywhere I went, so I figured it was purely a surveillance tail even if they were cops. The most disturbing question I had about it was not so much concerned with intentions as with origins: who were they?—why were they following me?—where and how had they gotten onto me?

Were these the same guys who'd been staking out my house, and had they somehow tracked me over here? Or had someone been watching Cherche's place? Or had they been alerted to my presence there from inside? I had stayed and talked with Cherche for about ten minutes after "Angélique" had been excused. Time enough, yeah. Dammit. I had to get some things settled.

So I found a coffee shop with off-street parking and watched the rearview carefully as I pulled in, saw the tail go immediateloy to the curb half a block to the rear. I parked where they could see me without too much strain, locked up, went inside and had some pie and coffee, then used the pay phone to call Tom Chase's home number.

I got his wife, Miriam, very uptight and not at all friendly. "What the hell are they doing to Tom?" I asked her, merely trying to verify that he had indeed been arrested.

"Nothing compared to what I'm going to do to him," was the angry reply. "Are you mixed up in this?"

I said, "God, I hope not. What is he charged with?"

She virtually spat it back at me: "Espionage."

"That's heavy," I said. "Does he have a lawyer?"

"I don't know about him, but I've sure got one!" she replied.

"What does that mean?"

"It means I'm filing for divorce, that's what it means. You should see the stuff they found in his car. Has he always been a pervert? Honestly, I've been married to a total stranger. I never knew this man! Have you known about this?"

I told her, "I don't know what you're talking about, Miriam. I doubt that you do either. Don't be hasty about—"

"Well what can I expect! Of course you'll defend him! You're exactly alike! All of you cops are the same! Don't call here any-more, Joe!"

She hung up in my ear but I didn't really mind. Miriam had always been an asshole in my book. Never could understand how Tom would put up with her, let alone kowtow to that kind of bitchiness. I always sort of thought that she was the main rea-son why Tom and I had drifted so far apart. She'd never liked me either, probably raised hell with him every time we got together.

So, what the hell, at least I was finding some reference in reality. It had not *all* been lies. Apparently Tom was indeed in custody and in deep trouble. I didn't know what to make of the "pervert" stuff but I figured it wouldn't take much to make a pervert of anyone in Miriam's eyes. I remembered how upset Tom had been over the possibility that she would learn of his involvement with another woman in the case and...

And what? That he'd been led along, suckered and fatally compromised by that woman? Was that what was happening to me?

I needed a bit more reference with reality.

So I left some money on the counter and went out through the kitchen, circled the block on foot, came up behind the tail car. Different car, yeah, and different guys. I shattered the window on the passenger side with the butt of the S&W, pulled the guy through the opening and bounced him off the sidewalk, almost had ahold of the other one but he'd kicked the starter damn quick and was screeching away from there while I was reaching in for him. I had to disengage cleanly or get my arms ripped off so I stepped away and let him go.

Had what I needed, anyway—someone to identify. This one was bloodied and groggy, harmless looking, total stranger. I helped him to his feet and hustled him up the street, pushed him into the van while onlookers gawked, got the hell away from there. The guy was groaning and dabbing at facial cuts with a handkerchief while I careened around the streets looking for another place to stop and interrogate. Found a deserted parking lot beside a bank several blocks over, opted for that.

I pushed the guy hard against the door on his side, wedged his head between the dash and the windshield, invited him to tell me all about it. Didn't take him long to decide that might be the most intelligent thing to do, but what he told me did not make me much happier about the reality we were referencing.

Seems that he worked for PowerTron as a security officer. Tom Chase was his boss but there were several layers of management between them, didn't know Chase personally, didn't know anything about his trouble with the feds. Didn't know Cherche LaFemme, didn't know any Gina Terrabona and had never heard the name before, had also never heard of Nicholas Gudgaloff.

I gave the guy some breathing room and handed him a first aid kit. Things got almost chummy after that. He treated his cuts while we continued getting acquainted.

"What is your interest in Joe Copp?"

"Never heard of him either."

"So why were you tailing him?"

"Oh!—is that you? My God, are you a cop? I didn't know..."

"Tell me about the tail."

"This is like moonlighting. I work for PowerTron but this is extra, personal work for Mr. Putnam."

I had to challenge the guy. "Who is Putnam?"

"He's the executive vice-president of the company."

"So how does personal work for Putnam put you on my tail?"

"They just gave us the description of the van and said we should keep tabs on it."

"When was this?"

"This was at six o'clock tonight."

"How did you know where to find me?"

"Not you, the van. They sent us to the address in Beverly Hills, said look for it then stay with it. We saw it going in and we stayed with it."

"You were keeping a log or something?"

"Yeah."

"Time in, time out?"

"That's right."

"You keep saying 'they.' They who?"

"Well...dispatch. Whoever is dispatching."

"You said this was personal work for Putnam."

"Right. I didn't mean official PowerTron dispatch. I don't talk to Putnam directly but..."

"So where is it dispatched from?"

"His house, maybe, I don't know. We have a radio in the car."

"PowerTron car?"

"Yeah."

"How many people involved in this?"

"What do you mean?"

"How many like you working directly for Putnam?"

"Oh. I don't know. Quite a few, I think."

"How many people in PowerTron security?"

"It's a big department. Several hundred, I guess, just at my plant. I mean, you know, it's three shifts plus all the clerical and administrative."

"So we're talking about a small army, if you put them all together from all the plants in the area."

"Probably a thousand people, yeah."

"Tom Chase headed all that?"

"Yes, he's director of security for the whole division."

"He's in jail."

"No!"

"Oh yeah. The feds took him in last night. Charged with espionage."

"Espionage!?"

"Yeah. How does that cut with you?"

"My God! I guess that explains why..."

"Why what?"

"Why Mr. Putnam took direct control of security."

"But you seemed to think you've been moonlighting."

"Well that's the way they made it sound, swore us to secrecy and all that, but..."

"But now you're seeing it differently."

"Yeah. God, what a bomb this is!"

I was beginning to see the faint dimensions of something far bigger than Chase himself had hinted at when I was recruited into the mess. And no comfort whatever for either Tom or myself.

As for Gina...

I did not want to think about Gina.

I took the guy back to the coffee shop and let him out. Didn't seem to be at all mad at me, even wished me good luck. I watched him inside, saw him head straight for the telephone. There was only one way in and out of the parking lot, so I circled the block and came back up the street, went to the curb at almost exactly the same spot the other guys had used to wait for me, had the place in good view.

It was a short wait. The same car came back from the opposite direction and made a left turn into the coffee shop lot. My pigeon came out immediately and entered the car, they went around the loop and came onto the street toward me. There was a lot of gabbing and arm waving as they went past totally absorbed in each other. I gave them a block then did a U-ey and fell in behind.

They led me straight to Pasadena via Coldwater Canyon and

the Ventura freeway, took about thirty minutes because it was not nine o'clock yet and traffic was still pretty heavy, took another ten minutes straight up Lake through Pasadena and Altadena into the high hills, so it was almost exactly nine when I cut the tail and reached for my briefcase to get Putnam's precise address. They could be headed nowhere else, and I didn't want to push my luck into those darkened hills with hardly any other traffic moving through.

So I gave the moonlighters five minutes then went on under my own lead.

It was a big joint, two storied with maybe an acre or two of grounds, gated entrance, circular drive, ablaze with lights everywhere. I left the van a block away and went back on foot, carrying the reloaded S&W in shoulder harness and a small backup pistol in the boot.

The car I'd been following was nowhere in sight. That should have told me something but I guess I was too focussed on slipping into the place unobserved. Two other cars were parked in front of a large garage and a third was standing under a portico at the entrance to the house. There were lights everywhere but no sign of human presence. I pushed the gate open and walked up the drive. Something got me to quivering because I had the S&W in hand as I went up the steps to the house. The front door was ajar. I went in, expecting and almost hoping to be challenged at any moment but there seemed to be no one at home.

I was wrong.

I found the ones at home in the library. One was crumpled just inside the door, a youngish man wearing a business suit he would never need again. An older man wearing silk pajamas and a dressing gown was collapsed in a chair behind the desk, deep in the sleep from which one never awakens.

These guys had been dead for quite a while.

I assumed that the man in the dressing gown was Morris Putnam, had no idea who the other stiff was and didn't especially care at the moment. My survival instinct was telling me to get the hell out of there quick but I guess the police instinct was stronger. I was searching through the desk drawers when the sheriffs made a grand entrance with weapons drawn and irresistible demands. I served with these guys for five years myself so I knew it was no time for idle debate.

I meekly took the spread right there at the desk. They took my guns without comment, and cuffed me.

There were no questions, no explanations.

This was one of those times when the right to remain silent should be vigorously exercised. It's a passive right, though, and damn small comfort when it's the only right you've got.

CHAPTER
TEN

THERE SHOULD have been reason enough to doubt that these people had been dead long enough to go stiff but their killer was still hanging around. But, see, police investigations do not ordinarily proceed on grounds of reasonable doubt. They leave that to the courts. The police take it by the numbers—not calculus but basic arithmetic—and what they see is what you get. An armed man standing over a dead body equals killer and victim, as simply as one plus one. Forget that "innocent until proven guilty" routine. That too is for the courts. Has nothing whatever to do with police procedure.

So I knew what I was in for. I was already wanted for questioning in connection with another killing, and possibly several more if they'd tied me to the freeway thing. Didn't take these guys any mental gymnastics whatever to come up with that score. Procedure is procedure, however, and it took us a long time to get there.

I'd figured that it was about nine o'clock when I arrived at the Putnam home, give or take five minutes. I sat outside in a police car until nearly ten, then I was taken down to the Altadena sub-station and sat around there for another hour awaiting transport to the county jail. I knew some of these guys, by sight if not by name, but that doesn't cut you any slack in a homicide. I wasn't treated badly but there were no special considerations either.

The booking procedure took forever. It was past midnight before the sergeant even came in and started writing it up. By then I was damned near a basket case. Every hurt I'd incurred over the previous twenty-four hours was making itself felt again, which did nothing to bolster a crumbling morale as the immensity of my problem began to settle on me.

Which is to say that I was feeling mean and nasty when the homicide team finally took it over. Those guys would have laughed me into a padded cell if I'd told them the story. So I told them nothing. They played the usual games—good guy, bad guy—bait and switch—derision and sympathy—but I remained surly and uncooperative through it all, and now it's two o'clock and I am dying inside.

That is where I was when the FBI took over.

They have a big contingent here in L.A., hundreds of agents and I don't know how many different departments but I know it is a damned big operation. The two who came in to talk to me looked and acted like senior people. Of course you never know with these guys. Talking to an FBI guy is like talking to a lawyer, in fact it's usually the same thing, so they all act like senior people.

These two wanted to talk about Walter Mathison, the one that tried to whack me at Gina's apartment. What did I know about him?—how long had I known him?—what was the connection with the Sarastova woman...?

They got to me on that one. I unbuttoned my lip at that point long enough to ask, "Who's she?"

She lived in the apartment in which Mathison was killed. What was my relationship with her? Was she a client? How long since I'd seen Thomas Chase? What was my present relationship with Chase? How long had I known Morris Putnam and George Delancey and what was my relationship with them? What did I know about a shooting on the freeway in which three men were killed?

I just glared at them through all of that. The one was a Special Agent Browning—did most of the talking—the other Special Agent Vasquez. Smooth as silk, both of them, but tough as hell also under that surface, and these are the kind of guys you want to worry about. So I told them nothing. I saw them huddling with the homicide team before they left. Shortly thereafter I was accorded my right to one telephone call, and it took another hour for my lawyer to arrive.

We have an arrangement, my lawyer and I. We work for each other as the need arises and all we pay each other is expenses. Works out to a pretty good balance for both of us, but I think he was a little afraid of this one.

"Jesus, Joe," he growled at me, "I think you've outdone yourself this time. These people are ready to throw the book at you."

I growled back, "Yeah, well, let them get in line. I've had everything else thrown at me today already."

He said, "Don't be flippant about this. You're in deep trouble. You'll have to spend at least the rest of the night in jail. How much bail could you go?"

"Try fifty cents."

"Get serious about this and do it damn quick. How much could you raise?"

So I got serious about it and we made a list of assets. Looked sort of pitiful, on paper like that. Equity in my house was by far the best thing I had going. Bondsmen demand at least ten percent in security up front. We figured I had ten percent of damned little, which can be demoralizing as hell when you realize that it is the net residue of your life's work.

"I'll see what I can do," the lawyer said worriedly, and left me on that note.

Now it is four o'clock and the "procedure" has run its course. I am strip-searched and taken to a holding cell. It is not all that bad, considering where I have been the past seven hours. This is not "justice" but we have not even reached that plateau yet. First comes a damn lot of abject humility.

YOU CAN be denied bail under our system if you've been accused of a heinous crime and someone can convince a judge that your release pending trial would constitute a menace to society. But judges are part of the "innocent until proven guilty" procedure so it's tough making something like that stick before the question of guilt has been decided. They are supposed to give the benefit of any doubt to your constitutional rights. So I knew I was in pretty deep when my lawyer came back at eleven o'clock that morning with the news that the prosecutor was demanding that I be retained without bail. The judge was going to announce his decision at one o'clock. Even if he ruled in our favor, he would probably impose a very high figure for bail, high enough that I would have to rot in jail until I got my day in court.

"How high would that be?" I wondered aloud.

"It could go to a million dollars."

I said, "I'll rot, yeah."

But it seemed that maybe I was being offered a deal by the prosecutor. If I would be more cooperative...

"What do they want?"

The lawyer acted a bit embarrassed. "It seems that there are national security implications, Joe. They want you to tell them what you've been doing, on whose behalf—where, when, all the details. I doubt that they will be satisfied until you've incriminated yourself in one area or another, that's my worry. I advise you to talk to them but in my presence only. Let's at least create the impression that you're trying to cooperate but control the damage all we can. If the deal falls through then at least I'll have something to take before the judge to argue for a reasonable bail."

"What exactly am I being charged with?" I asked.

"You don't know?"

"I was booked on suspicion of homicide, haven't seen the actual charges," I replied.

"Well they've got you for three."

I swallowed hard and said, "Okay."

"A Walter Mathison—who, incidentally, was a Special Agent of the FBI—a George Delancey and a Morris Putnam."

"That was Delancey, eh?"

"What do you know about these people, Joe?"

I said, "Not nearly enough to cop for their murders. I shot Mathison, sure, because he was shooting at me, but I didn't know at the time that he was FBI. The other two guys I just walked in on. Dammit, they were stiff already."

"The theory is that you came back to look for something."

"That's too dumb," I said. "I don't even know how they died."

"They were shot." He was looking at me hard and close. "With your gun."

I looked him back, harder and closer. "Neither of my guns had even been fired since..."

"Yeah?"

I said, "Oh shit."

"What?"

"A certain person walked away with one of my guns early yesterday. It was out of my hands until late last night, just before I went out to Putnam's house."

"All three men were killed with the same weapon, Joe. This gun that was out of your hands all day yesterday—was it by chance an odd-size big calibre?—a .41 Magnum Smith & Wesson?"

I sighed and said, "That's it."

"They have a ballistics match on it."

I said, "I'll talk."

The lawyer patted my hand and said, "I'll tell them," and went out of there quick.

Damn right I'd talk.

I would talk to anyone who would listen.

IT WAS quite a party. Present were two detectives from the sheriff's homicide team, a guy from LAPD, two prosecutors and the two FBI men, Browning and Vasquez. Plus me and my lawyer, of course, and a stenographer. The room was crowded and stuffy and I felt like a jerk. One of the prosecutors was a woman, pretty little thing with a sympathetic smile masking a mind of cold steel.

I told it pretty straight, beginning with the Sunday night meeting with Tom Chase and the illegal entry at the Russian consulate, my discovery and escape through the second story window. Browning wanted to know what I'd taken from Gudgaloff's office. I told them about the black book, explained that I'd had time to only glance inside to verify the contents and that it seemed to contain the information I'd been sent for.

Of course I told about the encounter with Gina outside the consulate but for some strange reason I covered her the best I could, said I didn't know her last name and that was not exactly a lie, explained how we'd spotted the police stakeout on my car so she'd offered to put me up for the night, told about the shoot-out at her apartment and my decision to take her to the mountain cabin.

The FBI guys wanted minute detail concerning Mathison. They kept interrupting, probing, trying their best to trip me up and make me admit that I had surprised Mathison in Gina's apartment and shot him cold. So I finally had to make a big deal out of the fact that I had not tried to conceal the shooting but had actually reported it by telephone to LAPD. I also pointed out that only two shots had been fired, one by me and one by Mathison, and his had buried itself in the wall beside my head right at the front door—so who had surprised whom, and where the hell was his authorization to enter that apartment anyway?

The chief prosecutor had to step in and break that up. I was invited to continue the story, which I did but without all the personal stuff between Gina and me. I just told them that we went to sleep and she was gone when I woke, also gone was my evidence and my pistol. I related the whole thing about being picked up on the mountain road by the people from the consulate, the CHP pullover and the quick switch between cars, the ensuing shoot-out on the freeway ramp. Again, here, I got into it with the FBI. I had to show them my cuts and bruises and they still couldn't believe that I had walked away from that if I had been inside the car with the victims.

The LAPD guy wanted a physical description of the CHP motorcycle officer who'd pulled us over while I was in the Russians' car. Who the hell can give a description like that? Those guys all look exactly alike, describe one and you describe them all. I asked if they couldn't get verification from the CHP but nobody volunteered to answer that so I went on with the story. Told them about my second encounter with Gina at my place and the third one in Beverly Hills—though I covered Cherche, too, all I could—how I got my gun back and how I busted the tail I picked up there. The FBI was all ears again as I related the PowerTron security connection but this time they let me continue without interruption.

The rest I told absolutely straight. They dismissed the stenographer when I finished it and then there was a long "off the record" discussion of my story between the principals and my lawyer. After that the FBI went into a huddle with the prosecutors just outside the door.

Then the chief prosecutor came back in and said to my lawyer, "Without stipulating to the veracity of anything your client has told us, we do recognize his exemplary past record as a police officer and we appreciate his willingness to cooperate with the investigation. Accordingly, we will recommend to the court that his bail be set at one million dollars."

Big deal.

But my lawyer thanked him and when we were alone again he turned to me with a big smile. "All *right*," he crowed. "Now we're getting somewhere."

We were getting nowhere that I could see.

"I still can't make bail," I told him.

"Sure you can." He dug into his briefcase and produced a bond commitment. "You already did. I was handed this right after I left you, a while ago."

I still didn't understand.

"Your friend put up her home this morning."

I said, "What friend is that?"

"Your friend in Beverly Hills," he said. "Mrs. Sarastova. The one you referred to in your statement as Cherche LaFemme."

It knocked the hell out of me, pal.

But it also knocked me back onto the streets. And I didn't know if that was a favor or not.

CHAPTER
ELEVEN

MAYBE YOU have a better handle on things at this point than I did while I was experiencing it, so maybe I'm looking sort of dumb to you right now and you are wondering why I didn't just hang it up and let the proper authorities unravel the thing. But remember that a lot of stuff was coming down and that a guy can get a bit shellshocked when he's in the middle of something like this. Give some credit, too, to the fact that I have been officially inside many such investigations over the years, so maybe I just don't have your confidence in the system. Sure, there is a tendency at such times to want to just crawl away and find some place safe and comfortable where you can lick your wounds, say to hell with it all, let things take their course. I thought of that, yeah. Trouble was, things were already taking their course and sweeping me along with it. Get swept into a cesspool, pal, and you'd better get busy trying to find a way out if you don't want to get buried in it, inch by creeping inch, while waiting for someone to come along and pull you out.

I could feel it creeping past my chin and knew that I had to get very busy indeed.

That does not mean that I knew the way out.

But I did know that I would rather swim than sink into that mess, so I started stroking.

We had determined that neither of my cars was in the impoundment yard, so I said goodbye to my lawyer on the jailhouse steps and took a cab to the last place I'd seen the Cadillac, since it was the closest. It was still there and still intact, with a wad of parking tickets lodged into the wiper well.

It started right up, and I drove straight to Cherche's joint in Beverly Hills. I thought it very bizarre that she would go my bail unless somehow that would serve her own best interests. We'd been friends, sure, but what she'd done was far above and beyond the call of the very tightest friendship and we were a long way from that.

I had it by official record now that her real name was Elena Sarastova and she owned the Beverly Hills property unencumbered except for this new lien by the bail bondsman. It was valued at two and a half mil—which just goes to show, girls, what one can get by just doing what one does best. The name had thrown me a bit because I'd already settled onto it as belonging to Gina, since the FBI agent had referred to Gina's apartment as "the Sarastova woman's" and also because of questions regarding the young lady's true identity.

So I had hoped to get the answers to several questions in Beverly Hills. As it turned out, I got quite a bit more than I was expecting, and also quite a bit less. What I got was a new client. What I did not get was a lot of comfort regarding my own situation.

IT WAS four o'clock in the afternoon and she was having breakfast beside the pool, looked about the same as the last time, dressed about the same—a remarkably good looking woman for any age. I accepted an invitation to join her with toast and coffee, and I'd had two cups of coffee and all the dry toast I can tolerate before another word was spoken. I guess each was waiting for the other to start. She outwaited me. Finally I said, "Thank you, Cherche."

She showed me a solemn little smile as she replied, "No thanks are necessary, Joseph. You know that I would share my breakfast with you any time."

"You know what I mean," I growled.

She leaned forward to lightly pinch my cheek, then shook it gently before letting it go. "Why are you always such a tough gorilla, my darling?"

"You should've seen me an hour ago," I told her. "Have you ever seen a gorilla cry?"

"I would like that very much," she replied teasingly.

"Want you to know I appreciate it."

"Very well, I know it. And . . . ?"

"And what?"

"What else did you come to say?"

"Don't know quite how to put it," I said uncomfortably. "But . . . why?"

She smiled at my discomfort and said, "Why not?"

"What do you want from me, Cherche?"

"Aha. The table is turned, is it not? Usually between us the question goes the other way."

I said, "Okay, so I owe you. How do I square it up?"

"You are a very good policeman, no?"

"I try to be."

"A very tough cop, they call you. How tough are you, Joseph?"

"Depends. Tough as I have to be, I guess. How tough do you need?"

"How tough is Mother Russia?"

I said, "I don't understand."

"She has been thought dead these many decades, or else totally dominated by those who raped her. But she is not dead, Joseph, and she is not the whore they thought her to be."

"Tough old broad, huh?"

"Exactly. Do you understand *perestroika?*"

I replied, "As a buzzword..."

"Buzzword in this country, perhaps—but, Joseph, in certain quarters it is seen as the re-awakening of the tough old broad. The USSR is not Mother Russia, and *perestroika* is no instrument of Soviet socialism. It is acknowledgement that socialism is unworkable and dying. Can you imagine Marx or Lenin advocating free enterprise in their day? No. And they are proven wrong."

I said, "I'm not much into world politics, Cherche."

"Nor am I," she replied. "But I want you to understand that I am not a communist."

"Never figured you were,"

"Good for you. But some perhaps think that I am."

"Why would they think that?"

"Because of my encouragement of Mother Russia. I am not political, Joseph, but I can be very sentimental. And I remember the stories told to me at my mother's knee. I would love to see things that way again in Russia, or at least the possibility that it could occur. Do you understand?"

I asked, "What does this have to do with me, Cherche?"

"Everything," she said quietly.

I took a deep breath and said, "Okay. What do you want from me?"

"Find out about Nicky for me."

"What about Nicky?"

"Is he Russian?—or is he Soviet?"

"It's not the same, eh?"

"In the heart, no, it is not the same."

"I was told that he is KGB."

"Yes, I know you told me that. I believed at the time that you were wrong."

"At the time?"

"Yes. If you were wrong, then all perhaps is well with me. But if you were right... then, Joseph, Cherche may be in need of a very tough gorilla."

"That's why you hocked your house?"

"What good is the house, darling, if Cherche is dead?"

I took another deep breath, let it go, told her on the growl, "A lot of people are dead already, darling."

"This I know," she said quietly. "Save me, Joseph."

"Just like that, eh?"

"Save me."

"You'll have to help me do that."

"Very well."

"That means total honesty."

"Of course."

But she was lying in her teeth already. I don't believe she ever intended to give me even ten percent honesty. I sort of sensed it at the time, but I had to give the lady the benefit of any doubt. She'd hocked a mansion to get my sorry butt out of jail. So I owed the lady one very tough gorilla.

I just hoped the hell I could find one.

CHAPTER
TWELVE

CHERCHE WANTED me to attend a "very special party" at her place that night, assuring me that we would have ample opportunity to talk during that event and also hinting that I would meet some interesting people there. Meanwhile she had many things to do in preparation for the event and wanted to be left alone. I later learned that she throws those "very special" parties almost every night. It is basically how she makes her living, so this was just business as usual and she was trying to fit me into the routine without disturbing it.

I needed the time anyway. Wanted to check on my van and find a way to get it back home and tucked away, also there were things inside it that I needed. I stopped at a U-Haul on my way through Pasadena and rented a tow bar, found the van in good shape, towed it home. Things seemed normal there too. I put the van in the garage and double-checked the premises before I went into the house.

All was shipshape inside so I threw a frozen dinner into the microwave and ate it in the study while reviewing the papers that Tom Chase had given me earlier. Found nothing that meant much more than it had at the start, except I noted that both of the murdered PowerTron executives had families and I had to wonder about the survivors. Wondered also about the circumstances at the Putnam home that allowed his death to go undiscovered those many hours.

The cops had been very cagey about all that, gave me no information whatever concerning time of death or anything else. But if the men had been killed with my gun, and if death had occurred prior to my second encounter with Gina—which was the next time I'd seen the gun—then Putnam and Delancey had apparently lain dead since some time in the early afternoon. If I had been the first to discover the bodies, then why were all the lights on inside and out?—and where were the families of these men during all this?

If, on the other hand, death had occurred after that afternoon encounter with Gina, then the timeframe could narrow somewhat and maybe all the lights had been on because it was dark or getting that way and Putnam had been expecting company. That would put quite a squeeze on, though, because I'd hit Beverly Hills at nightfall and obviously both Gina and the gun were there when I got there. Since I'd left home shortly after the encounter with Gina and went as straight to Beverly Hills as I could under the circumstances, that would not seem to leave her much time for a swing through the Altadena hills, and since the gun had been in her possession both times...

No, I had to go with death in the afternoon.

I had to wonder, then, about the PowerTron security cops who'd tailed me away from Beverly Hills. The guy I busted had told me that he was moonlighting for Putnam, that he was being "dispatched" privately by someone under Putnam's direct control—and they had made tracks straight toward Putnam's place after I let the guy go.

Had I given those guys enough time to discover the bodies, turn on all the lights and get the hell away from there before my arrival?—and could that account for the presence of the sheriffs minutes after my arrival on the scene? But why would they run through the house turning on all the lights, either before or after the discovery? If before, would that be any way to act in their boss's house?—and why do it afterward if they did not mean to report the crime and hang around until the cops arrived?

But wait... what or who sent them up there to begin with? The guy said they were radio dispatched. The one must have called it in when I pulled his partner out of the car. When I let the partner go, I saw him go straight to the telephone and the same car came along minutes later and picked him up, so that sounds like a dispatch. Then they hightailed it for Altadena. Why? And if they found the stiffs, who would they report it to? —and who would have ordered them to get the hell away from there before the cops came?

There was much to be considered, see, and it did not all necessarily revolve around Gina. Then again, it could. Now she had flat-out told me that she worked for PowerTron and Tom Chase. No mistake about that. Even told me that she got the job via her Pentagon connections. So where did she fit into all this? Could it be that she worked for PowerTron but *not* for Tom Chase?

My lawyer had been trying to get a line on Chase while I was in jail. No way. The feds had him under tight wraps, virtually incommunicado. We couldn't even get a line on his lawyer, if he had one, and it seemed likely that, based on past experience with these guys in similar situations, they were moving him around from one federal facility to another in an attempt to keep him buried in the system. They can get away with stuff like that, sure, especially when there is a "national security" cover for it.

So I had damn little hope of getting any information from Tom in any foreseeable future. Which is to say, in any useful future. Time was closing in on us, I was certain of that. I couldn't afford to just sit around and wait for the feds to remember the Constitution, so I had to write Tom off as a source of useful information in the meaningful future. I was alone in the mess and I knew it. And most of what I had—even from Tom himself, maybe—was either misinformation or disinformation.

See I'd been set up by Tom himself to leap to conclusions concerning Gina when he hinted that a woman was involved in his problem. You remember what he told me, and you've seen how his wife Miriam reacted to his arrest. Gina herself had helped strengthen the perception by her emotional show of concern for Tom and her apparent determination to "build the case" for him. But what if she'd been building a case *against* him? What if she'd been working for Putnam all along?

And what if she was really working for Nicky?

Why had she taken my gun?—and then why had she been so determined to give it back? Had she come to my house that afternoon merely to plant a murder weapon to incriminate me? —and had she then seized a golden opportunity to doubly incriminate me by luring me to that house in the hills with the murder weapon on me? What was her real connection with Cherche, and why had Cherche hocked her home to get me on the streets again?

These were things to ponder.

Believe me, I was pondering like crazy while I cleaned up, dressed up, and set off for the party in Beverly Hills. It was, I hoped, going to be a very interesting night.

S OMETHING HAD been nagging at my lower mind all evening so I stopped along the way to make a call from a public telephone. A cool female voice responded to the first ring with a very controlled, "Putnam residence, Mary speaking."

I didn't know from Mary but it figured to be housekeeper, family, or close friend at such a time. According to my record, Mrs. Putnam's name was Barbara. So I asked Mary, in the same sober tones, "How is Barbara doing?"

"Much better now, thank you," said Mary. "Could I tell her that you called?"

"Please," I replied. "Just tell her Joe. When is the funeral?"

"We're not sure yet. Not all of the family has been notified so it's still up in the air. Call again in the morning. We should know more by then."

I followed a wild hunch to ask, "Do the kids know?"

"Yes. We found Beth finally. Her group had taken a side trip from London to Stonehenge, but she called just a few hours ago. She'll be back tomorrow."

I glanced at my poop sheet. "How is Morris Junior taking it?"

"Well now he is head of the family, isn't he? I believe that he is the only thing keeping his mother sane right now," Mary replied chattily, warming to me. "He won't be returning to UCLA until —well, for a while."

"Must have been devastating for Barb to find out that way," I guessed again.

"Well, yes, she just couldn't get it out of her mind that he'd been lying here dead while she was partying in Aspen. But she's coming to grips with it. Thank you for calling, Joe. I'm sure it will be a comfort to her."

"She may not remember, I just met her in Aspen. But tell her anyway."

Mary's voice was tinged with an unspoken question as she replied to that. "Oh, of course, I'm sure she will remember. Are you...in town now? Coming for the funeral?"

I said, "No, probably not, it's a private time, I respect that. Just tell her I called. And uh..."

"Yes?"

"Well I was wondering about Toni Delancey. Have you heard...?"

"Oh, you're with the company."

"Not exactly, but..."

"Yes, Toni came by today, she's okay, quite a trooper. She's planning cremation for George as soon as the authorities release the body."

I said, "You're quite a trooper too, Mary. Thank you very much."

That voice was warm and almost intimate as she said good-bye. "Thank you too, Joe. Come see us when it's convenient."

With that tone of voice, she could have meant "safe" instead of "convenient." I'd heard it before, that tone, when women share delicious secrets. So what kind of partying, I wondered, had Barbara Putnam been enjoying in Aspen while her husband lay dead?—and how tight a marriage could it have been if the impression was accurate and the death and burial of a husband was a mere inconvenience?

But of course I could have been entirely off base on that. I had called merely to satisfy the curiosity about why the bodies had not been discovered before I stumbled onto them. Apparently I had the answer to that. Wife vacationing in Aspen, daughter apparently touring Europe with a group, son living on campus at UCLA.

But now I had to call the other widow. Just had to.

Damned glad I did, too.

I recognized the voice, you see.

Had just a light touch of very soft accent, one of those indeterminate foreign touches that can be so very pleasing when the mood and the moment is right.

It was not all that pleasing this time but I recognized it with the first hello.

I disguised my own voice the best I could as I inquired, "Mrs. Delancey?"

"Yes. Is this Mr. Williams?"

"Yes. How can I . . . ?"

"I must leave for Europe as quickly as possible. How much longer must my husband's body be detained?"

I guessed that she'd been expecting a call-back.

But I did not know what to tell the lady about her husband's body so I merely hung up the phone and went on to the party.

But something else had been settled, as well. Gina's name was not Terrabona or Sarastova or even Gina. It seemed that her official name would turn out to be Toni Delancey, and wasn't that a shocker.

CHAPTER
THIRTEEN

IT IS quite a large place, sits well back off the street behind high walls and even higher shrubberies in a solid atmosphere of inpenetrable wealth, swankily private. Best little whorehouse in Beverly Hills, bet on that, and with strictly a carriage trade. The automobile gate was standing open and two pleasant looking young men in tuxedos were manning it. Both were eyeing the old Cad a bit nervously until I identified myself, then I was waved through with a proper flourish and I checked the car with a valet at the front door.

The Cad got tucked into very good company already assembled there—I figured maybe a million bucks in rolling stock, allowing fifteen grand per wheel—and I was ushered into the entry hall where two more tuxes eyeballed me, checked me off a list, and passed me on through.

Inside, it looked like any other high society cocktail gig you might find anywhere. Ladies in flowing gowns and gentlemen in black tie stood about in small groups engaged in genteel conversation, uniformed waiters moving restlessly, bearing silver trays ladened with interesting fingerfoods and drinks—forty to fifty people, at quick estimate, about evenly divided between male and female. That translated to no less than twenty johns, and the evening was very young.

Found myself wondering how much my pass was worth, decided that Cherche knew whereof she spake—I couldn't afford Angélique or anyone else in this joint—and I wondered why she'd wanted me there. The smooth blonde whom she'd introduced as her secretary came over and took my arm, stopped a waiter and hospitably urged me to partake of the rich offerings. I said no, thanks, I'd had a TV dinner, but I accepted a glass of wine just to show that I was no party pooper.

"Where's the party?" I asked her, looking around at it.

She showed me a smile that contained a secret and stepped closer to murmur, "Depends. We call this room our depressurization chamber. Mostly, first-timers are brought in here. Gives them a chance to, you know, acclimatize just a bit."

I said, "Uh-huh. Then what?"

"Depends," she repeated.

"On what?"

"On what it takes to fully please our guest. Where would you like to go from here?"

"What's on the program?" I asked, genuinely curious.

"That's up to you, isn't it?"

"Is it?"

"Sure. Whatever you'd like. You'll find young ladies in the game room if you'd like to just sit and talk, get better acquainted with someone, whatever."

I asked, "Are all these girls . . . ?"

"Hostesses, yes. Take your pick."

"That would be like a kid in a candy store," I told her. I gave her a closer look, then, and asked, "How 'bout you?"

She smiled and said, "That would have to, uh, be arranged in advance. I am generally not included in the pick."

"Like Cherche?"

She rolled her head to one side and gave me a sidewise gaze. "Sort of like that," she said soberly.

"And Angélique?"

"Uh-huh."

"Is she here tonight?"

"Angélique? I'm not sure. Later, perhaps."

I kept trying. "Suppose I don't see a girl here who turns me on?"

"Then you're in real trouble, aren't you," she replied with a teasing smile.

"Let's say that I am."

"Is this for real, or... ?"

She excused herself quickly to greet two new arrivals, distinguished looking men in their sixties, chatted with them briefly then passed them off to another girl, rejoined me with an apology. "Sorry. What were we—? oh yes, we—"

"Cherche asked me here for a reason. I think I know now what the reason is. She wants me to see her operation. So why don't we just get to that."

She gave me a briefly speculative eye then took my hand and walked me toward a door at the far side of the room. "Sex is like food," she told me as we were getting there. "There is hot dog sex and gourmet sex. You can get a hot dog on any corner. But if you want fine cuisine..."

We'd stepped into a broad hallway. It was carpeted and decorated with fine art.

"...usually you'll want to see a menu, first."

A ladies powder room was just down the hall. We were headed that way.

"Of course, those who demand the best are usually prepared to pay for the best. We cater to the gourmet appetite. And we specialize in full course meals with all the trimmings."

She'd stopped me at a door next to the ladies' room, opened it invitingly.

"You could find an appetizer in here, or perhaps simply an intimate look at a particular dish. Careful, you may find it a bit dark at first. I can't go inside with you but I will be nearby when you are ready to leave."

I went in and she closed the door firmly behind me. It wasn't all that dark, just a twilight effect—long narrow room with easy chairs lined up at a trick mirror, you know the kind, mirror on one side but transparent from the other, and of course this was the transparent side. Two men were sitting there in total silence, one of them nervously puffing on a cigarette, watching two girls primping at the mirror.

It was just a game, of course. The girls knew the guys were there but were acting like they didn't, and they were helping each other with their hair and cosmetics, adjusting their bras and fooling around with their hosiery, that kind of stuff. I knew where it was headed so I stepped back outside.

There were trick-mirror "appetizers" all over the joint, de-signed for varied tastes, but I sampled only one more—it was quite enough, really—featuring a guy and two gals in a live sex show.

For some people, I figured, the appetizer would be the entire meal. For myself, I always figured sexplay as a participator sport and I said as much to my guide.

She shrugged and told me, "You may participate as you wish, but not here. This house is merely the kitchen."

I said, "Oh. It's carry-out."

She said, "Yes. Except by special arrangement."

"What could be specially arranged? A room upstairs?"

"Yes. Or..."

"Or what?"

"Special parties."

"Here?"

"Uh-huh. Game room, and at the pool."

I said, "But I could take one of these girls home with me to-night."

She rolled that oblique gaze at me again. "Or one of them could take you home."

That gave me a glimmer. Maybe it explained why "Sarastova" was the occupant of record at the apartment where I'd had the encounter with Walter Mathison. I didn't voice it, just tucked the thought away for future reference.

"You could also arrange a video taping," my guide informed me.

"Why would I want to do that?"

She delicately shrugged, showed me that secret smile, replied, "I am told that it can be a powerful aphrodisiac to re-live one's most powerful fantasies, to be the star in one's own porno-graphic film."

I told her, "What I keep seeing here is bundles and bundles of money."

"Well, we are not selling hot dogs here. We do not cater to that trade. For those to whom we do cater, the cost is secondary and probably inconsequential. What is a few thousand dollars to these men who deal daily in millions?"

I suggested, "You could be selling total disaster to some of these people if the truth came out, though. These are big men. They must be nuts to risk..."

We were standing outside the game room, beside the pool. It was a warm night and the moon was high. She placed a hand on my shoulder and asked me, "Can I tell you a trade secret, Joe?"

I said, "I'm always game for those."

"The bigger the men," she told me, "the bigger the demand for our kind of services. And these men did not get where they are through timidity. You think these men are afraid of risks?"

"I guess you're right," I said. "But there's such a thing as plain stupidity too."

"Not where sex is concerned."

"No?"

"No. Especially not when it is the only gratification left."

I asked her, "Do all you girls talk this good?"

"We can talk any way our guests desire. Would you like me to get down and dirty?"

I chuckled and told her, "I couldn't afford it."

She laughed, too, and told me right back, "Oh, I think you could."

"Really?"

"Catch me on a good day."

"Is this a good day?"

"This is a terrible day. Introductory nights are but once a month and require exhaustive preparation. It is very tiring."

"That's what this is? All first-timers?"

"Yes. It is like a showcase. Mainly what we sell tonight is stock."

"Stock? Like shares?"

"Sort of like that, except they do not pay dividends. Well, not *cash* dividends."

"It's a club," I guessed.

"A company," she corrected me. "Money passes hands no other way and we sell nothing but stock. The dividends may be taken however and whenever the member chooses."

"Quite a wrinkle," I commented, ". . . for the oldest profession."

"Oh it is not the oldest," she said.

"No?"

"No. Not even the most enduring."

"What is?"

"Dominance," she said soberly.

"Think so?"

"Oh absolutely. Without dominance there could never be prostitution." She inclined her head toward the game room. "These men here—these big men—theirs is the oldest and most enduring profession."

I figured probably she had something there.

On reflection later, I knew damn well she did. They owned us all, guys like these did, in one fine way or another, and they manipulated us all according to their needs.

It was a whorehouse lesson for me, and I would never forget it.

It even helped move me toward the resolution of this case.

CHAPTER
FOURTEEN

THE DUMBEST whores in the world have a view of us men that is quite unlike any we could ever have of ourselves. They get us at our best and our worst, our strongest and our weakest, and they know us in very special ways. The dumb ones maybe cannot verbally express that knowledge in any coherent way, but when you get a smart whore—an intelligent, educated, refined whore—then you're just so much clear glass, pal, whether you've slept with her or not.

I did a lot of time as a vice cop so I think I'm speaking with some authority on the subject. I've dealt with them all, from the fourteen-year-old runaway druggies hustling cars from street-corners to the aristocratic madams such as Cherche who consort with world leaders, and I have to feel that any natural woman in any walk of life could become a whore in certain situations. I forget who said it but some very wise man has been quoted as saying that every woman has at least a bit of whore in her, and I think he meant it as a compliment. Maybe I wouldn't go that far, but of course a lot depends on what you mean by the term.

I have known whores who do it as a hobby, not from financial necessity but just for fun. I have known a few who did it merely to cover their own indiscriminate appetite for sex, and I have suspected one or two of doing it because really they hate men and see it as a way of cutting them down to size. For most, though, it is simply a means to an end, a business, and many of those feel in no way degraded by their business.

Cherche's operation was sort of unique not only in the way she worked it but also because of the quality of her women. There were no kids here, no druggies, no dummies. These women could have made it anywhere, in any calling. They were bright, well-educated, mature, personable, highly attractive, classy. So why did they become whores? I don't know why because that is something that you just don't ask, so I stopped asking it a long time ago, especially of whores like these.

The "secretary" was called Alexandra. That is her professional name and all these women here had great names like that. She was solid class from head to toe, and I have already exposed you to her depth of thought. To "buy into" this company, a guy had to submit a financial statement and undergo a severe background check. I gathered that the women were selected just as carefully. They were medically certified "safe" on a regular schedule —and it was my understanding that the examining doctors were also "stockholders" in the company, so their own good health could have been at stake in those checkups.

Each woman had her own apartment around town and the rent was paid by the company; some senior women lived in condos owned by the company. Personal relationships with outside men were severely frowned upon, and they definitely "worked" for no one but the company. The lifestyle was high, as provided primarily by the company, and the direct salary excellent, with an equivalent amount invested on the woman's behalf in solid portfolios.

I didn't get all this in one piece, of course, and I give it to you here merely as background and to show that your perception of whoring may not exactly fit the circumstances here.

Alexandra was quality stuff, like "Angélique"—who, by the way, obviously did not fit the employee profile if what I thought I knew about her was true—as were all of them I encountered that night. Cherche, of course, was in a class by herself, the brains and heart of the whole operation—and Cherche was centered somehow in all the problems confronting me at the moment. I knew that, or at least sensed it, so I was not just dallying among the lilacs in that visit to Beverly Hills that night. Don't think I was somehow immune to the very powerful sexual aura of the place, I was not—but it was a time for work, not play, and I was working every damned thing I could at the moment.

I was left to my own devices for about an hour, just nosed around on my own—an obviously square peg in this gathering of millionaires—and tried to keep out of the way. One white-haired gentleman did accost me and bluntly asked who I was and what I was doing there. I replied that I was seeing to his security and he made a remark to the effect that I should have been in black tie like everyone else—wouldn't stand out so. I told him that my tie was at the cleaners and promised to wear it next time. That drew a short laugh but he kept eyeing me in a way that made me uncomfortable—I was beginning to feel like a dividend—so I was glad for more than one reason when I was finally summoned to Cherche's apartment, which occupied an entire wing upstairs.

It was designed and fit for royalty, of course, and Cherche looked totally at home in the midst of that. There was a lot of red in silks and velvets, an equal amount of black in laces and leathers—the hot-cold, yin-yang of sexual opposites in every touch and look—and some of the most startling pornographic art in both canvas and statuary as these jaded eyes have ever seen, truly masterworks from around the world and obviously worth a fortune.

This of course was merely the sitting room and there was ample comfort for a dozen sitters. I didn't see the bedroom except a glimpse through a curtained doorway suggesting more of the same in there.

My hostess wore silk lounging pajamas all in one piece with a plunge in front to the navel and slits up both legs above the knees, red and black of course. I wondered what it must be like to live one's entire life, night and day, encapsulated within such frankly erotic surroundings and I wondered how much of this catered to Cherche's inner world and how much to the outer, decided that I would probably never know.

Didn't have much time to think about it anyway, as anything more than a passing quiver, because there was so much more to command the mind at the moment.

Ivan the Terrible was there, too, see, in company with two other ironjaws and a fourth man who could only be Nicky the Great. All four were in black tie and it was easy to understand why Cherche had laughed at me when I told her that Gudgaloff was a KGB chief. Looking at him now for the first time I decided that if I was casting movies, I'd type this guy more as a French gigolo, or as a playboy at the courts of Europe—too pretty, for sure, to play at cloak and dagger. He was a well set up guy, though, I would say of aristocratic bearing and carriage, very handsome with jet-black curly hair, good teeth that showed a lot because he smiled a lot, a perhaps deceptively friendly gaze.

Cherche introduced us and immediately withdrew, as though it had been planned that way although her excuse was that she needed to greet some important guests downstairs. Ivan shook me down clean, he and his ironjaws retreated into the background of the large room, and then it was just Nicky and me.

He said, in perfect British accents, "You have been a busy man, Mr. Copp."

"Call me Joe."

"Good! Call me Nicky."

I said, "Not busy enough, Nicky. 'Busied' probably is the better word."

He laughed, and it was a pleasant enough sound. "Or 'harried,' perhaps."

"Yeah," I said. "And damn near buried."

"It is good to see that you do not easily lose your sense of humor. You will no doubt need a lot of that in the coming days. Do you understand what has been going on with you?"

I replied, "Sure. I stole something from you and now you want it back. You could've just asked, you know, except that someone else stole it from me and I can't give it back."

"Why did you take it?"

"I was paid to take it."

"By whom?"

"Sorry, Nicky, it would be a breach of professional ethics to tell you that. You understand."

"Honor among thieves?" he asked, with one eyebrow raised.

"Something like that," I allowed.

"We don't want to hurt you, Joe."

"Don't, then," I suggested.

"We are modern men, in modern times. There exists a tension between us. Let's release that tension, and perhaps we can be friends. Who paid you to burglarize my consulate? Where is my property now?"

I said, "You just don't get it, do you. I am not going to tell you who hired me and I don't know where your property is. If I did know, maybe I'd tell you and maybe I wouldn't."

"Why did you come to Cherche?"

"I've known Cherche for a long time," I replied. "I spotted her name in your book. Little while later I had to kill a man in self-defense. I needed to know why, and Cherche was the only clue I had."

"I see. And what of Tom Chase?"

"What about him?"

"You brought up his name."

"I used to know a guy by that name," I said.

He waved a finger in front of his nose and asked, "But what was the relevance to Cherche?"

I shrugged and replied, "No relevance at all, apparently. Her Tom Chase and my Tom Chase are not the same. Told her that."

"Yes I know, but . . . what I mean . . ." He was waving the finger again. ". . . where did you learn of Cherche's Tom Chase?"

"She told me."

"No. First, you asked her about Tom Chase. You asked her."

"Right, and she told me he's from Israel. Wrong guy. My Tom—"

"Please stop this, Joe! Where is Tom Chase now?"

"Beats me," I said.

"Why did you inquire about him?"

"The name came up."

"When you were hired to rifle my office?"

"Maybe. Or shortly before or after, I don't remember. Hey, I was grasping at straws."

"Were you employed by the FBI?"

"You kidding?"

"Were you employed by PowerTron?"

"Why would they?—oh, I see what you're getting at. I didn't

kill those guys, Nicky. I just blundered into it a long time after the fact and the sheriffs came in and found me there. I think I was set up."

"Set up by whom?"

I said, "That's what I'm hoping to find out, pal."

"And what will you do if you find out?"

I smiled a crafty smile, I think, as I replied to that. "I might kick some ass. Then I might hand over what's left to the cops as a substitute for my own ass. Do you have any suggestions to help me do that, Nicky?"

He smiled back, crafty for damn sure. "If one comes to me, I will let you know."

Cherche returned at that point in the conversation. She showed me a dazzling smile then turned immediately to Nicky to inform him, "Angélique is here."

He held out a hand to me and I shook it. It was not one of those really friendly grips but it did not seem hostile or uninvolved either. Call it an understanding handshake, between two guys who pretty much have each other's number—a shake of mutual respect. To be sure, I had already revised my initial reading of the guy.

This was no gigolo.

Maybe I would cast him as a crown prince.

He and his retinue departed immediately. I presumed that he had been waiting for Angélique. So was I, in a way, although I could hardly picture it if Angélique was also Toni Delancey, waiting to bury her murdered husband.

But it is, what the hell, a crazy world after all.

CHAPTER
FIFTEEN

ONE STRONG impression that I got from that meeting with Nicholas Gudgaloff was that he seemed as much in the dark as I was concerning the events of the past few days. Either that or he'd just been playing it dumb and pushing my buttons for effect, but I'd also sensed an element of fear in that interchange, experienced as extreme caution or delicacy out of place. And that had me wondering.

As soon as he and his people left the apartment, Cherche turned to me with a troubled smile to ask, "So now what do you think of my Nicky, darling?"

I told her, "You'll be the first to know, darling, when I find out. Next time you're going to deliver me into the hands of my enemies, though, give me a little warning, huh?"

She took it with pained innocence. "But I did not deliver you,

Joseph. I assumed that you wished to meet with him. It is he who was delivered. He telephoned earlier for an appointment with Angélique. I instructed him to meet her here, thinking it the perfect opportunity for you."

"We'll talk about it later," I said impatiently. "Right now I need a word or two with Angélique."

"That would not be possible," Cherche informed me, with a disapproving shake of her head. "Angélique awaits Nicky in his car."

"Where are they going?"

Another disapproving shake, and: "Not tonight, Joseph."

I jumped right into her face, I guess, because she drew back with a start as I replied, "Don't give me that delicate business bullshit, Cherche! That girl is with the lions, not the lambs! Where are they headed?"

She merely shook her head in distressed silence. I beat it out of there quick and got outside just in time to see a stretch limousine and a following car pull away and circle toward the gate. I was delayed then by a brief altercation with the parking valet, who wanted me to observe the formalities and allow him to fetch my car. I gave him a buck and a push and fetched for myself, hit the gate about ten seconds behind the others, and picked them up a couple of blocks along.

It was easy to keep them in sight—maybe too easy, I thought a couple of times—as we wound north to Sunset and then sedately westward. The hour was late, close to midnight, and the traffic was light and almost leisurely. The track led past Bel Air and Brentwood, on beyond Pacific Palisades and then northward along the coast highway toward Malibu. I was beginning to wonder if the chauffeur of that limousine had been instructed to just meander around and kill time—if, you know, the party or whatever was inside the limo itself. That filled my head with non-tantalizing thoughts which made me realize that I did really care for that girl, whoever the hell she was and whatever her role might be in all this intrigue. It seemed obvious that Ivan and his thugs were following the limo in the accompanying car, so that would leave plenty of intimate stretch in the back seat for Nicky. And it was bothering the hell out of me, yeah.

They pulled into a small roadside shopping park on the approach to Malibu where there was a small liquor store and market. I was laying back a good distance so I didn't see what transpired there. They were moving again within a minute, and this time with a bit more zip to the trip.

I hoped they were not headed for the Malibu Beach Colony. It's a very ritzy settlement on the sands for the rich and famous with controlled access and I'd have a hell of a time getting in there. So I was thankful when the track turned into the hills and ended there.

The apparent destination was a rather unimposing homesite that had been scooped from the plunging mountainside to make a little "ranchette" with stables and corral, spectacular ocean view, lots of eucalyptus and exotic shrubbery. You could just barely see the place from the roadway and I would have missed it entirely if I had not been in position to see the other cars veer away at that point. I was far behind and running without lights, and I pulled over immediately and killed the engine, went the rest of the way on foot since there was absolutely no traffic up this way and I did not wish to advertise my presence.

The house was set below the roadway, accessed by a narrow lane that wound down to it. Lights were showing down there as a diffused glow through the vegetation. I could hear snatches of soft music and I smelled the evidence of horses nearby, if you know what I mean. There are horses out my way, too, and I live with that smell when the wind is wrong.

I cased the place as best I could from the roadway, then ventured in via the corral fencing and felt my way around to the stables and a small parking area just beyond. I could hear men talking somewhere out there and quickly determined that it was coming from the access lane uprange. Cars were parked all along there, maybe six to eight all told, and four more in the stables area. So it was evidently a gathering of some kind, maybe a party and maybe something else.

Turned out to be both.

Apparently some of those cars assembled there came with chauffeurs, who were having their own little party outside. I managed to catch a glimpse of big Ivan and his thugs at the periphery of that outside gathering and I got the impression that they were tensely aloof from the others. Maybe it was just a language barrier and maybe it was something else. Whatever, that glimpse served as warning that I should not get too fancy with my footwork on this turf.

I worked my way around the far side of the house, taking full advantage of the darkness and foliage in which it was set. The view from the front was spectacular, yeah—both ways, from the house and into the house. The whole front wall was glass and there was a deep patio area extending in a semi-circle to the very front edge of the property with nothing but a low split-rail fence to keep you from stepping off into thin air.

This was the area, I remembered, where the foundations of very expensive houses occasionally slide down the mountainside. I could see why, and I would not want to be inside this one in a heavy rain.

I had worked my way into some shrubbery about twenty feet from the house and had a pretty good view into the large room at the front. The only tux I saw was on Prince Nicky and he looked very out of place in that crowd. Most of what I saw were faded denims and T-shirts, on male and female alike, and I guess there were fifteen to twenty people in that room. I did not see

Gina-Angélique-Toni right away, but I did see another familiar face in that crowd—and it gave me quite a pause.

I had not seen the guy face to face for several years but there was no doubt that this was one Frank Dostell, an infamous Hollywood insider once referred to as "the Pusher to the Stars." The guy dealt in cocaine and everyone knew it. He'd been charged several times but never convicted, never even brought to trial. Some of us cops used to sit around the table and wonder out loud who was running interference for Dostell. It had to be someone big, someone with political clout, and maybe that is why there was never heart enough among the cops to pursue the matter.

Anyway, Dostell's presence here was a shiver for me, even though it might mean nothing whatever to the overall weave of my present problem. You don't forget a guy like Dostell, and you never get over the frustration of seeing someone like this strutting around and thumbing his nose at the law.

While I was looking at him, this time, Gudgaloff took him by the arm and drew him aside in a sober conversation. That's when I spotted Angélique, dressed in a devastating skintight white sheath that weighed maybe eight ounces and measured no more than twenty inches overall. She slid open a patio door and stepped outside, stood there for a moment just sort of sniffing the air, then sauntered out to the railing at the overlook.

She was close enough at that point that I could almost reach out and touch her. I watched the house for a moment to be sure that no one was joining her outside, then I spoke to her, very quietly, from my cover.

"Don't react, don't look around."

She didn't, but the tremor in her voice told the tale of sudden emotion as she gasped, "Joe! Are you crazy?"

"Sure I'm crazy. So are you, kid. What's going down here?"

"It's just a party!"

"Is this Dostell's place?"

"No. A film director lives here, Dan somebody. What are you *doing*?"

"Watching your ass, pal, that's what. Are you okay?"

"Of course I'm okay! Get away from here!"

"In a minute. You're in terrible company, kid. What brought you here?"

"Frank Dostell."

"Yeah?"

"Yes. Nicky searched for him by telephone from the car. He located him here, so on we came. Why does it matter?"

"Maybe it doesn't," I told her. "Then again...do you know what this guy is into?"

"I know, yes. And at the moment it also is what Nicky is into. He can act quite irrationally at such times. Know what I mean?"

"He's hooked on the stuff?"

"I think he is hooked, yes."

I said, "Well, well."

It was a powerfully seductive idea, almost a stunning idea. A KGB station chief? Hooked on cocaine?

"Please get away from here, Joe. Do not be concerned for me. I can handle Nicky."

I said, very soberly, "Guess you can, at that. You can handle any man, can't you, Toni?"

I'd placed heavy emphasis on the name, and it hit home. She sort of drooped and leaned against the rail, took a deep breath before replying to that shot. The voice was entirely flat as she said, "So now you know it all."

Maybe it would have been easier if we'd been standing toe to toe, eye to eye. This way it was just cold and weird, me speaking to her backside while she spoke to the Malibu wind. "I know a lot more than I understand, kid. Any time you want to sort it out for me..."

After a moment she replied, "I did not know about the gun, Joe."

I said, "That's okay, I didn't know about Putnam and Delancey either. How'd they get shot with my gun?"

"This I do not know. It was in my possession all that day, but I shot no one. Especially I did not shoot..."

Her husband, yeah. I'd been wondering about that and I had to ask her about it. "Who do you think did it?"

"Someone with very good reason, I would say."

"Uh-huh. Well...my condolences, for what it's worth."

"I stopped grieving for lost love a very long time ago," she said with a tremor in the voice.

I said, "Okay."

"George and I separated quite a long time ago."

"Okay."

"So it was you who called earlier tonight, not the man from the morgue."

I said, "Yeh."

"Do you hate me?"

I said it, and meant it at the moment. "I don't hate you, kid."

"That is good. Because I have been thinking since yesterday that perhaps I have found love again."

I said, as tough as I could say it, "Don't count on that, pal."

That cost me a ton of agony, I'll level with you.

Maybe it cost her something, too. She straightened up, said, "Very well, pal," and marched back inside.

There have been times, I'm sure, when I have felt worse than that. But I could not remember any of them.

I tried to shrug the feeling off as I cautiously made my withdrawal and returned to my car.

I did have, after all, some very tantalizing ideas to play with.

Trouble was, my heart did not want to play with them. Gina, Angélique, Toni—whatever the name, my heart that night had its own agenda.

And that is about as deep as you can get, pal.

CHAPTER
SIXTEEN

EVER NOTICED how time can expand or contract at certain times to manipulate our sense of reality? The hours I had spent with Toni that spanned our first meeting outside the consulate on Tuesday night and my awakening alone at the mountain retreat on Wednesday morning had seemed like a fingersnap of time while I was experiencing them, yet those meager hours contained practically all of my direct experience of her and in retrospect they seemed a lifetime. I had to keep working the time through my mind to keep the reality in grip. This was Thursday night. Tom Chase had contacted me on Sunday night and I'd invaded the consulate on Tuesday night. So this was merely Thursday of the same week and that did not add up to anything like a lifetime, yet the feeling was there.

I have been married several times, and each time for several years. Each marriage contained some good and some bad times and I had never regarded any of them with bitterness. But all those years and women combined could not add up to mean as much in the sensing of my life as those few hours spent with Toni. I did not understand it and I did not like it, but there it was anyway.

I was giving it a lot of thought as I whiled away the night in my car beside that Malibu mountain road. I was positioned in good enough cover with a good enough view of the roadway and I had a night 'scope which would help me pick out faces in the darkened interiors of cars passing by, and of course I was waiting for a particular face to come my way.

Gudgaloff and crew were the first to pass, about thirty minutes after I'd begun the wait. I sent a mental salute to Toni and let them pass. Twenty minutes later another car came down, and then another shortly thereafter, but I waited until two o'clock for Frank Dostell. He was driving a hot looking Ferrari and a woman was in the seat beside him. I gave it ten seconds and pulled out behind him and took up the track. Wasn't a very long one. Ended at a beach house several miles along the highway toward L.A., one of those that are jammed in side by side with backsides and garages butted directly onto the highway.

I made a mental note of the location and went on by as he was wheeling the Ferrari into the garage. By the time I got turned around and found a place to park, lights were on inside the house and I could hear angry voices raised against each other as I felt my way toward the ocean side. These places are built for maximum exposure to surf and sand. Every year, it seems like, when the winter storms come in across the Pacific, the houses along here get battered and flooded and one or two washed away, but you couldn't pay these people to live somewhere else.

Don't blame them, it is nice if you can afford the lifestyle and don't mind the roaring of surf night and day.

This one had open decks on two levels overhanging the sands, stairways from both levels—maybe a duplex, up and down— glass fronts for maximum ocean view. The lights and sounds were on the lower level. I reached the deck outside just in time to witness a full blown domestic brawl, assuming they were married or living together.

Dostell is about my age, I guess, give or take a couple years, suave looking guy with military hair and mustache, glittering eyes that can go real mean real quick—probably handsome and sexy from the female point of view. He had no visible means of support other than investments in movie properties from time to time—films, that is, with occasionally a credit as a co-producer —and I guess he had backed a couple of small local plays that had gone to Broadway and made some bucks for him. He made it look good on paper, anyway, and kept his illicit gains very well covered.

There had never been a suggestion from any source that Dostell was into big time drug trafficking but it was common knowledge among the in-crowd that he had all the necessary contacts and an ever available access to cocaine, which had become the glamour drug of the eighties. Cocaine from Dostell, in fact, had greased many a business transaction in the local movie and music communities while greasing his own slide into the inner circles of local wealth and power as well.

Of course, most of this had come during those naive years when all the hip people were deluding themselves with the thought that cocaine was a harmless ride into fun and frolic, in a town that does love to frolic. The drug's proscription was viewed as a ridiculous and misguided attitude of the square community, much the same as the prohibition of alcohol in an earlier era, and those who were brave enough to deal in the stuff were accorded no less respect than the bootlegger or speakeasy proprietor of yesteryear.

In fact, Frank Dostell had been a very popular hero of the drug revolt and apparently he continued to wield considerable influence even during this enlightened time. Part of the reason for that, of course, was that so many who had lionized him in the past were now addicts and relied on his continued good favor to feed their habits.

I have seen so much of this, you know. I've seen what an addiction can do to deservedly proud and successful people and the depths into which they will descend in order to safeguard their supply of the junk. Which is why I was so intrigued with the possibility that Nicholas Gudgaloff might be caught in one of those descending spirals. If it could happen to bankers and generals and movie stars and recording stars and athletes and all the other bright people of our age, then why not to a bright and ambitious Russian agent far from home?

Which is exactly what I wanted to discuss with Frank Dostell.

Though there were drapes at that glass wall overlooking the sea, they had not been drawn and my view was through lacy curtains which really did not hide a lot from up close. I could hear the angry voices even over the sounds of the surf but I could not distinguish words. The woman was not a bad looker and seemed quite a bit younger than Dostell. She had a nasty mouth, though, and she was screaming things at him apparently at the top of her voice, judging by the body language that accompanied it. He was yelling back at her and pacing around the room. It ended, finally, when he began slapping the hell out of her and tearing at her clothing.

I had no part in that. I simply held my ground there in the shadows of the deck and waited for a chance to get closer. Don't know to this day what it was all about and didn't really care at the time. They kissed and apparently made up with her standing naked in his arms, then she gathered her clothing and went into another part of the house.

Dostell made himself a drink at the bar and came out onto the deck, walked right past me to stand at the rail and gaze broodingly at the sparkling surf.

I could not have set it up better myself.

"Won't find your answers out there, Frank," I told him from behind.

He turned on me with a startled face; asked, "Who the hell is that?"

"Doesn't matter who it is," I replied. "It's purely business."

"What kind of business?"

"The life and death kind. Yours and mine."

"Everybody dies," he said quietly, almost thoughtfully. I was shadowed by the building and he was trying to get a better look at me.

"Some sooner than others, though," I reminded him, "and some harder than others. Lately there's been an epidemic of hard and premature deaths. I think one of those is trying to find you. Me for sure."

"Who are you?" He was circling warily, squinting in the effort to pierce the shadows that enveloped me. "You look familiar."

"I should," I told him. "I busted you once."

That really pissed him. Those glittery eyes were blazing with hatred as he growled, "I won't tolerate this kind of harassment! I'll have your Goddamned badge! What do you—?"

I stopped him with a very simple device, the snout of a pistol. It was in his mouth before he even saw it and his last few words were biting on it. The taste and feel of it locked his jaws in place and bulged the glittery eyes.

I told him, "The name is Copp, with two 'p's. I haven't been a one-P cop since shortly after the first time we met, so I've had no

interest in people like you. Suddenly I've got a new interest because it seems my life is at stake. Way it works out, that puts
your life on the line with mine. I'm not going to play cute games
with you because there's not time enough for that and because I
don't like you very much, Frank, to start with."

It was a long speech to bear with one's mouth wrapped around
the cold steel of a revolver. He was beginning to drool around it
already and I still had a few words to say up front.

"We begin with the self-evident truths and go on from there.
I'll ask you a simple question. Then I'll give you the opportunity
to give me a simple answer. We'll try that first, see how it goes.
It's up to you, Frank. How long have you known Gudgaloff?"

I withdrew the barrel of the pistol but let the muzzle nestle
the lips and made him speak past it. Very effective arrangement.

"I think since shortly after he came here." Dostell replied
shakily into the pistol bore, all the fight drained out of him. "Five
or six months, I guess."

I gave him some cold steel to suck on while I asked the next
question, then again withdrew it to the muzzle for his reply. We
did it that way every time, so the conversational flow was not as
smooth as it may seem here.

"Did he find you, or vice versa?"

"He found me."

"How?"

"A party somewhere. He just came over and said he'd like to
buy some stuff."

"He's quite the party animal, eh?"

"I guess so. He makes buys usually two or three times a
month."

"Expensive lots?"

"Usually, yes."

"Is he a user?"

"I think so. But no one could use that much."

"What does he do with the rest of it?"

"I think he gives it to his friends."

"Or business associates?"

"Well, that's usually the way..."

"What?"

"I said usually that's how it works."

"Why is that?"

"Well...that's how...this stuff is power, you know, it's better than money."

"Gives one a business advantage. Do that for me and I will do this for you."

"Yes. Look do we have to—?"

I gave him enough barrel to gag the most determined fellatrix and said, "Uh-uh—I ask, you respond. Did he make a buy tonight?"

"Tonight? Uh..."

I reinserted the barrel of the revolver as I told him, "That was a test question, Frankie, and you failed it. Try again."

"I saw him just a few hours ago."

"For a buy."

"Yes."

"And what else?"

"Well, he...wanted to know...if I'd thought it over."

"Thought what over?"

"Uh..."

I said, "I'm not sure how many tests I will let you fail, Frankie."

"Our proposed business venture."

"*Perestroika* venture?"

"Yes."

"Exports to Russia?"

"Yes."

"In particular, the commodities that are at your disposal?"

"Yes."

"How?"

"Uh..."

"Last chance to make me happy, Frankie."

"They have diplomatic privileges."

The woman surprised me at the doorway, hadn't heard her come up and apparently she had not been aware of my presence either until she was almost on top of us. She let out a gasp and a little squeal, and Dostell made an appealing gesture toward her, like trying to calm her. She was still naked but had added a few trinkets to emphasize the nudity.

I was about out of questions anyway.

I withdrew the revolver as I told him, "Congratulations, you passed this time."

Then I vaulted over the railing onto the sand below and got the hell away from there.

All in all, it had been a highly profitable night. Not only did I have a possible KGB cokehead, maybe now I also had a KGB official trying to smuggle the junk into the very square Soviet Union via diplomatic pouches.

So now what the hell could I do with that?

CHAPTER
SEVENTEEN

RIGHT AWAY there was a problem with Gudgaloff. Had to do with image and the way our perceptions of the world here in America are distorted by our entertainment media. James Bond is sophisticated and classy, see, a good-looking womanizer and hip man of the world. But he is one of ours and apparently this is the vision we enjoy for our heroes. It is a perception of glamour and excitement that must fit well into the American image.

But we don't often see the other side that way. Not the KGB, especially. They tend to have shaved heads and brutish features, and they are very dull boys—sexless, humorless—with absolute and total allegiance to Marxist-Leninist goals and ideals. And it's not just the KGB image, this is the way we tend to see all Russians, as peasants and laborers—a nation of working-class stiffs

—toiling along with empty dreams and fruitless lives, unless they can make it in ballet or Olympic sports.

So that was the first problem with "Nicky" Gudgaloff. This guy was a true James Bond type working for the other side. He traveled around in a limousine, wore tuxedoes, mingled in high society and gained access to the in-crowds, consorted with business leaders and educators, spoke at trade conferences and farm granges, was becoming a familiar figure at every gala in town.

I had to believe that the guy had the full support of his government in all that. So was it *glasnost,* openness, and *perestroika,* capitalistic-style free enterprise, or was it merely a new approach to old goals for the Soviet Union? Hell, I did not know the answer to that and I could not afford to even wonder about it. Politics is not my game, especially not world politics.

But since my life was on the line here, I did have to consider and try to decipher the political implications if Gudgaloff had fallen prey to what older leaders in Moscow have termed "western decadence." I did not know, for example—is there a drug problem in Russia? Can the stuff be obtained as easily as here? If not, and if one of their officials comes over here and becomes a junkie—what happens when he returns home and his supply is cut off?

I remembered hearing something a few years earlier about an alcoholism problem in Russia—something, too, about a mental health problem centered on manic-depression and a high suicide rate. They'd also had their problems with black marketing and official corruption—inevitable, I guess, in a nation where the basic necessities are always in short supply.

I also remembered being surprised recently to learn that although Russia is a military superpower it is economically a third world nation, with per capita income about one-fifth of ours.

So what? So, okay, maybe "western decadence" is just a sour-grapes look at our culture from the other side, an officially "square" look that is trying to make the best of a bad situation at home—and maybe these guys feel like they've finally been let out of jail when they draw an assignment to these shores—and maybe some of them go a little crazy with it.

Maybe that explained our Nicky.

On the other hand, maybe not.

With my life maybe in the balance, I knew that I could not afford to guess wrong on this one.

I WENT straight back to Cherche's. The night was nearly over, though, and the place was buttoned up, gate closed, electronic locks set. I had to call in on the intercom to get through the gate, and that required a couple of minutes to get cleared through.

Several expensive cars remained in the parking area. I left mine at the front door. A youngster in waiter's attire let me in and led me back to the game room. He immediately went behind the bar and resumed a cleanup that apparently had been interrupted by my arrival.

Cherche came in before I got sat down. She'd changed outfits while I was gone, now wore long pendant earrings of diamonds and rubies, looked like, matching necklace with a pendant below the breasts, satiny spike-heeled evening slippers and a red see-through chemise or whatever, to about mid-thigh. That is absolutely all she was wearing, and it was immediately and entirely obvious that she wore nothing beneath that chemise.

She stretched up to clasp her hands behind my neck, and her first words were, "Why have we never made love, my darling?"

"One thing and another," I suggested, "probably got in the way."

"Ah, but there must be a deeper reason. Such a strong and virile man, my Joseph, yet so straight and unyielding in your judgments. I saw it when first we met, and I said to myself, 'Well, perhaps one day this one shall have wisdom and sensitivity to match his strength, then we shall see.' But then you went away, and I always wondered. Have you grown up, Joseph?"

"Probably not," I replied. "But you had it wrong then so you maybe have it wrong now. It's a matter of priorities with me, not moral judgments and certainly not disinterest. A matter of moment, darling."

I guess she became aware of my physical response to her close presence because she rubbed against me ever so delicately as she said, "Well then perhaps the moment has found us at last. A few guests remain overnight but they are in proper care and pose no concern. But you look so tired. Let me take you to my bedchamber and I will give you a nice massage, remove the frowns from your face. Then we shall explore our moment."

I am sure there was genuine regret in my voice as I responded to that offer. "What I need most right now, Cherche, is a moment of pure honesty and cold conversation. We all could be in very grave danger and there may not be a lot of time to prepare for it. Will you talk to me?"

She released me and stepped back, gave me a pouty little look, then turned to the bartender and quietly commanded, "Go home, Jimmy."

He needed to hear it only once, dropping a towel immediately and departing with a faint, "G'night."

I went behind the bar and poured several fingers of bourbon into a water glass, added ice, took it to a stool and perched there while Cherche watched in obvious agitation.

"Start at the start," I suggested bluntly, "but this time with total honesty. Tell me about Nicky. No—first, tell me about Angélique. Exactly who is she and how does she figure into your operation?"

"I have told you, Joseph, that she is the daughter of an old friend."

"That's what you told me, yeah. Try again."

She showed a quick smile and a sly look, came over and slid onto a stool beside me, kicked off a shoe and insinuated the bare foot onto my lap. "Always the policeman," she said playfully.

"Be glad of that," I recommended.

"Very well. You are right. I repeated a lie when I told you that. I knew that she was an imposter. But I know why, I think, and so I..."

"Go on."

"Well...the girl she claims—this girl died five years ago in Israel, the victim of a terrorist attack. This I know to be true. But..."

"But?"

"Joseph...would I disappoint you terribly if I tell you—you said that Nicky is KGB and I laughed when you told me that. Now perhaps you will laugh at me when I say that Angélique, I think, is CIA."

I didn't laugh, nor did I feel like laughing.

I said, "But you've known all along that Nicky is KGB."

"No. He came to me as a trade attaché seeking important connections, and he presented himself as a distant cousin. I have verified it. He is the grandson of my great-uncle on my mother's side. I have seen nothing of KGB in Nicky. But then when Angélique came to me...well, you see, it is a natural conclusion. And—this may disappoint you—I have had CIA contacts in the past. When you and I were friends in San Francisco, my darling, even then Cherche was a friend also to the CIA."

"You little devil," I said.

"Yes." She was enjoying it. "I took care of their fears and they took care of mine, you see."

"That explains your Bay Area clout."

"Yes, and the Southern California clout as well, at first. But that ended when the CIA became a national embarrassment, you see. There had been no contact for some time when Angélique showed up at my doorstep with this obviously false story. So I took her in, thinking... well, that I would give her time to reveal herself. There was initially the tiny fear, of course, that she could be working undercover for the police but... well, let's just say that I have no reason to fear that kind of intrigue. I am well protected, Joseph. The police are not my enemies."

"Do you know her true name?"

"No."

"Had you ever heard of a man named George Delancey?"

Cherche's face fell. "Yes."

"A client?"

"Yes."

"And Morris Putnam?"

"Yes."

"They're the guys I was accused of killing, you know."

"Yes, I know."

"Did you ever have any reason to tie Angélique to either of those men?"

"Oh no. They were gone before she appeared."

"Gone?"

"We cancelled their membership."

"We?"

"I and my board of directors."

"It's that formal, eh?"

"Oh yes."

"Why did you cancel them?"

"They were found to be undesirable."

"In what way?"

"They were not nice to the employees."

"You can put it straighter than that."

"These men, Joseph, enjoyed inflicting pain. We can cater and we do cater to the sublimation of that desire through games of pretense, but these men were not long satisfied with that. They injured some of our girls. We kicked them out."

"When was this?"

"Perhaps six months ago. I could look it up if the exact time is important."

I waved it away. "Maybe later. Tell me about Tom Chase."

She delicately shrugged and poked at me with her foot. "Angélique brought him. So I did not even check him out. By this time I had asked her about the CIA. She had not denied it. So, when she brought Thomas... and she hinted Mossad."

Well, that brought a sigh. The Mossad is the Israeli equivalent of the CIA and KGB. It was getting nutty as hell. Keystone Cops kind of nutty.

I said, "Dammit, Cherche."

She shrugged again and said, "So I began to wonder then if Nicky was in trouble at home, you see."

"Why would you wonder about that?"

"Well, he has been so nervous lately. And it had been very obvious to me that Angélique had set her cap for Nicky when first she came."

"When did you first meet Tom Chase?"

She screwed up her face to think about it, replied, "This was about two weeks ago."

"Tell me again that thing about Nicky. You thought he was in trouble because..."

"Well, yes, because you see he was also the center of attention for Thomas, and this made Nicky very nervous. He confided to me—Nicky, I mean—he told me that he may be returning to

Moscow one day soon because of the bad company that was attaching to him."

"Bad company?"

"Yes, and I assumed Thomas Chase to be the company of which he spoke. Nicky feared that his usefulness in this country would soon be questioned. When I pressed Angélique on this issue, she promised me that Nicky was not the focus of their investigation."

"Wait, wait a minute, Cherche. Angélique actually told you that—"

"No no, not quite that direct. She merely reassured me that Nicky was in no danger because of Thomas, that other matters concerned Thomas, business matters, and that he merely hoped to gain business access in Russia."

"But you said 'investigation'—that's what you said, the focus of their investigation."

"Yes, well, you see . . . I knew that they were together in an investigation because I am well familiar with CIA."

I said, "Jesus, Cherche, why are you giving me this line of bullshit?"

That hurt her, if her face was honest about it.

But I guess it wasn't the "moment" for me to get the full, unvarnished truth from Cherche.

The young bartender came stumbling back into the room at that very instant.

He had blood all over his shirt and his eyes were wild.

"I need help!" he gasped. "She's hurt!—bad hurt!"

"Who's hurt?" I growled.

The kid was about to pass out. "Angélique," he croaked. "At the gate. She's . . ."

I was already on the run.

As a "moment," this one had become a total disaster.

CHAPTER
EIGHTEEN

SHE WAS more bloodied than damaged, though someone had obviously beaten the hell out of her, and I found her staggering along the walk toward the house in a daze.

I scooped her up and carried her inside. Cherche and the kid, Jimmy, met us at the door and steered me upstairs to Cherche's apartment. We cut the bloodied white sheath off of her and put her to bed, then I went to work with cold compresses to staunch the bleeding and hopefully to control the swelling around the eyes and lips.

I'd seen worse beatings, much worse—suffered a few myself —but there's something particularly pitiful about this kind of damage to any woman, and I had an emotional involvement with this one, so the feelings were really intense.

I was glad that Cherche was there. She is a strong woman—I mean internally strong—and knew exactly how to handle the situation. I figured she'd handled similar situations in the past. She again sent the bartender home and took full charge. I gladly yielded my role as medic and stepped back to give her room with the patient.

She carefully cleaned the hurts and examined each one closely, then told her, "Not so bad, darling. This will mend. And if there are scars, then these can be made to disappear as well. Do not be concerned for that."

Toni had said not a word, and she responded to that prognosis with eyes only, a tired fluttering that seemed to be saying, "Just leave me alone, please."

She had not wished to talk to me or anyone else at the moment, that much had been clear. I could understand and respect that. Getting beat up is a lot like getting raped, to a woman, and maybe it's exactly the same. I'd seen enough of it in an official capacity to have become sensitive to the feeling, something like a sense of shame or degradation. I understood it.

Cherche pulled me into the sitting room and told me, "Not to worry, Joseph. I think there is no need for medical attention, which would be better in our situation. But I shall watch her closely, never fear, and I will not hesitate to summon help if that seems wise."

I growled, "I last saw her with your Nicky, just a few hours ago. I want his home address."

She gave me about a ten-second, unreadable stare, then went to a desk and consulted her personal directory, scribbled an address on a card and brought it to me. "Do nothing foolish, Joseph. These things occur. She will mend and forget."

"Not me," I muttered, and went out of there without further ado.

I AM not a "bad ass." People have called me that all my life, but it's not true. I'm as housebroken as any man I know and I really have a very gentle nature when people leave it alone. I never bullied and I never trespassed on another man's turf except when the need was unavoidable and the reason was clear. I've always been conscious of my size and strength, never liked to throw it around or to intimidate with it unless maybe that could take the pressure off a more dangerous situation.

But there do come those times now and then in a man's life when he feels plain *baaad* and the civilized constraints lose all meaning in the overpowering need to kick some ass.

The address Cherche gave me was one of the glitzy new highrise apartment buildings on Wilshire, and the bad was growing in me all the way there. I flipped my private badge at the doorman and growled, "Security inspection," in a tone not to be denied and went right on through without giving him a chance to think about it.

It was five A.M. and nothing was stirring but me as I punched the elevator to the sixteenth floor, found the door with the right number, leaned on the button of a built-in intercom and held it down until someone responded. I could feel eyes on me, spotted the little circle near the intercom that was the lens of a closed-circuit television system. I looked at it hard and said, "Open up."

A thickly accented male voice growled back, "Go away."

"The hell I will," I told it, and started kicking at the door.

It was beginning to splinter when I heard the mechanism moving and Big Ivan threw the door open. I read no hospitality in that angry gaze so I just kept right on kicking, first to the groin and then to the chin. That did not put him all the way down so I tried another to the groin and two more to the chin. That put him on his back. I stepped across and went on through, found Nicky standing in a bedroom door in pajamas and robe, alert and worried. He had a little auto in his right hand, one of the smaller calibres, and it was pointed my way.

I told him, "You'd better be an expert marksman with that thing, expert enough to place a shot squarely between my eyes or else directly into the heart. Because if you're not, I'll have that thing shoved down your gullet before you can get off a second."

He replied in tones meant to reassure, "Why would I shoot you, Joe? I believed we had an intruder."

"You believed right, that's what you've got. I came to talk about Angélique."

"At this hour? Couldn't it wait?"

"Not really. I just put her to bed, at this hour. She was very badly used, Nicky. That upsets me a lot. I do hate to leap to conclusions, but you're the last one I saw her with. Now she's damaged. I came to damage you back, if you're the one."

He looked genuinely distressed at the news more so than the threat, said something under his breath in a language I don't understand, then asked, "What happened?"

"She was beat up and dropped at Cherche's gate."

Gudgaloff came on into the living room and rather absently deposited his gun on a table, dropped into a chair, said, "I did not do that, Joe."

I had to believe it.

But I still felt bad.

Ivan the Terrible had struggled onto his knees and closed the front door, came lumbering over in a half crouch, misery in the eyes; he felt bad too, yeah. He also looked a bit confused and was seeking direction from his boss.

I asked Gudgaloff, "Does he speak English?"

"Very little," was the dispirited reply.

"Tell him I'm sorry. He should've been more hospitable. I'll make it up to him somehow."

The KGB chief gave me a small smile then relayed the message in appropriate lingo. He must have said more than that, too, because Ivan went out without a glance at me.

"That's twice," Nicky said to me with the same small smile. "I fear you can never make it up. Ilyitch is a very proud man."

"That's his name? He's Ivan the Terrible to me. Tell him I said that. And tell him I'm the kick-boxing champion of North America."

"Are you?"

"No. But tell 'im anyway, maybe it'll salve his pride."

"Very well. But what of Angélique? Is she badly hurt?"

"Mostly where it doesn't show," I told him. "But she won't feel like kissing anyone for a while. Lip's busted, eyes are a mess. She wasn't like that when you left her?"

"Of course not. She was perfectly well."

"When was that?"

"Shortly after two o'clock. She asked me to drop her at a house in Brentwood Park. I watched her go inside and then I departed."

"Remember the address?"

"No. She...did not give an address, merely directed the way."

"Could you find it again?"

"I could not, no. Perhaps my driver..."

"Call him."

He gave me a go to hell look but seemed to think twice about it, went to the telephone, spoke with someone very briefly, came back and told me, "Off the San Diego freeway at Montana, west to Woodburn, turn right the second corner, somewhere near the middle of the block on the left side, a white frame cottage with brick posts and planters."

I jotted it down and said, "I'll look into it."

"Will you let me know what you discover?"

"Sure. Did you notice if she rang the doorbell or...?"

"It appeared that she admitted herself."

"How long have you known Frank Dostell?"

He was like thunderstruck for a moment. He got up then and went to a desk, found a cigarette and lit it, didn't offer one to me, just blew the smoke back at me as he said, "That is none of your business, Joe. How do I make friends with you if you persist in...?"

I said, "Your secrets are safe with me, Nicky, if you're not using them against me. Why did your boys pick me up Wednesday morning?"

He frowned but replied, "You were the miscreant. I wanted my property. And I wished to talk to you concerning your reasons for taking it."

"How did you know where to find me?"

"Can we have a mutually advantageous dialogue, Joe?"

I said, "Sure."

"Very well. We knew where to find you because we knew where to find Angélique. Now you tell me—"

"No, hold it, that's only half an answer. Doesn't qualify. How did you know where to find Angélique?"

He studied my face for a moment, then replied, "Angélique had been under surveillance."

"Had been?"

"Yes. Since—well, that's another question, for later. Now my turn. Why did you take my property?"

I helped myself to one of his cigarettes but didn't light it, just let it dangle from my lips. Sometimes that's almost as good as lighting up when it's all stress and no action. "Someone hoped it would keep his ass out of jail."

"Did it?"

"Apparently not."

"I see. So where is the property now?"

I sucked on the dead cigarette for a couple of seconds, then told him, "I think the feds have it."

"The FBI?"

"Yeah."

That was unhappy news indeed for our Nicky. He didn't seem to know how to continue immediately so I figured it was my turn again. "On the way into town that morning, the feds pulled us over and I transferred to their car."

"Is that when they took the property?"

"No, before that. If you had Angélique under surveillance, how come your boys didn't stick with her instead of hanging around and waiting for me?"

"It took them a while to locate Angélique. By then..."

"Locate? First you say surveillance and now you say locate. Are we talking electronic surveillance?"

He smiled. "Very perceptive. Yes. There was a tracking device on her car."

I said, "That's bully. So you had two cars out there."

"Yes."

"And shortly after I transferred to the FBI car, that second car came alongside and blew it off the freeway."

"You have that wrong, Joe."

"Sure about that?"

"I am sure about that. The second car was already back in Los Angeles and keeping Angélique in sight."

"Why?"

He shrugged. "She was acting highly suspicious."

"What did you think she was up to?"

The KGB chief sighed, ground his cigarette into an ashtray, gave me a sad look as he replied, "The agent of my destruction, perhaps."

"How so?"

"There are enemies even at home, Joe."

"You talking about Moscow?"

He sighed again and this time looked even sadder. "I may need political asylum. Could you help me with that?"

I told him, "I don't know, pal. I think right now what we need is an insane asylum."

But none of us were crazy.

It just seemed that way.

The unfortunately violent encounter with Ivan had drained off most of my rage but I guess I was still a bomb looking for a place to explode. Difference was now, I think I was more angry at myself, and I believe I was beginning to develop some anger at Toni, too, at that point. I knew that I had to unravel the mystery of her and that I had to be prepared to deal with what finally fell out as raw truth.

So I made what peace I could with the Russians and went on to the next front.

CHAPTER
NINETEEN

IT WAS a quiet, modest neighborhood of custom homes on the west side of Los Angeles that had been developed probably forty years earlier—sort of upper middle class, I'd say, and no evidence of deterioration. The streets were narrow and straight, tree-lined, and the houses occupied fairsized lots with plenty of well-tended vegetation. American Dream made manifest, Los Angeles style. It was called Brentwood Park and enjoyed a reputation as one of the nicer abodes of the not-quite rich and famous.

I got there in early daylight with a sack of doughnuts and a carton of coffee, located the "white frame cottage with brick posts and planters," took station at the curb several houses down and across, and settled into the wait. I was expecting everything and nothing while trying to get mentally prepared for anything, spotted movement over there with the second doughnut as an automatic garage door opened and a car came backing out, quickly decided I hadn't been mentally prepared for this.

Had a perfect view of the face through that car window as it arced across in front of me, recognized it instantly, did not know exactly what to do with it but decided I'd better do something so I followed the car away from there and it led me to a restaurant on San Vicente, about five minutes away. I sat there still well-welling it and watched the guy park and go inside, then I did the same.

Seemed the only logical thing to do.

I slid into the booth across from him without announcement or invitation. His eyes jerked at me but there was no other visible reaction as he looked up from his menu. The waitress brought me one but I shook my head at her and said, "Just coffee. I ate outside."

She smiled at me and went to fetch the coffee.

Special Agent Browning put down his menu and said to me, "You're out early, Copp. Or is it just the tail end of a long night?"

"Both," I replied.

"Figures." He was eyeing me distastefully. "You look terrible."

"Feel worse," I assured him.

The waitress interrupted it with coffee for both of us. Browning ordered a waffle. When we were alone again, he asked me in a cold voice, "What do you want?"

"Guess I want to live to retirement age," I replied. "How 'bout you?"

"Is that a threat?"

I raised eyebrows at him. "Had nothing like that in mind, but..."

"But what?"

"Maybe a friendly warning. I think things are getting to a crunch. What do you think?"

"Too much crunch already," he replied sourly. "Get to it, Copp. I didn't invite you for breakfast."

"Toni Delancey got the hell beat out of her this morning."

That brought another jerk of the eyes, but all he said was, "Why are you telling me?"

I looked at the smoothly manicured FBI hands and said, "I've never hit a woman. Does it hurt the hand as much as hitting a man?"

He growled, "Careful, you son of a bitch. Don't start that crap with me."

I said, "If I'd wanted to start some crap, Browning, you'd be sitting on the sidewalk in a shower of plate glass by now. What is it with you FBI guys? Don't they teach civil manners at J. Edgar Hoover University? Most difficult bastards to work with I ever tried. Was Hoover gay?"

He showed me about one half of a very tense smile as he replied, "I couldn't say. You've got a smart mouth for a two-bit P.I. accused of multiple homicides."

"Not smart enough, obviously, to keep me out of this mess."

"And the one before that, and the one before that, and . . ."

I said, "So it's the hazards of the game."

I was sensing a bit of a thaw even before he told me, "I'll have to admit, Copp, that you do usually play a pretty tight game. Our file on you is thicker than any I've ever encountered for a peace officer. What are you trying to prove?—no, never mind, don't tell me. Let's keep it simple and pointed. What do you want from me?"

"Cooperation. As you noted, I'm accused of terrible crimes. I am not guilty of any terrible crimes. I did pull the trigger on Mathison but I did not know who he was at the time and I had absolutely no options. He pulled on me first, without warning and without provocation. What's your connection with Toni Delancey?"

He showed me a bit more smile and said, "I like the way you leap from one line of thought to another. That's very effective."

I told him, "I figured Gudgaloff was responsible, but he told me that he dropped her at your place at about two o'clock this morning."

"When did he tell you that?"

"About five."

"Uh-huh. And of course you believed him."

"Had to."

"What did you say happened?"

"Someone beat her and dropped her from a car, somewhere around four o'clock."

"Is she hospitalized?"

"No. A friend has taken her in. She'll get over it, I guess. Not sure I will."

"Who did she say did it?"

"Didn't feel much like talking, I guess, didn't say. We'll get to it, I'm sure. Meanwhile I've got this sleep disorder, can't seem to close my eyes with all this crap clinging to me. I can't wait for Toni to tell me about it. So I was hoping that you and I could..."

He was giving me the silent stare, kept on doing that while the waitress brought his waffle and topped off the coffee cups. Then he turned his attention to the breakfast and had eaten about half of the waffle before he said to me, in an almost civil tone, "It's a very convoluted case, Joe. I'm not sure that I could or should do anything at all to give you aid and comfort. But I'll think about it. Go home and get some sleep. Call me at the office this afternoon. Then we'll see what can be done."

It almost disarmed me, but not entirely. I bluntly told him, "Some of your people are kinky."

"Can you back up that statement with hard facts?"

"Not yet, but I'm working on that. You'd better start working on it too if you don't want to get eaten by it. Who ordered my arrest Wednesday morning?"

"I did."

"Why?"

"Because we had you going in. We knew that Chase had involved you. We knew that you had burgled the Soviet consulate. We knew that you shot Walt Mathison. And we'd known from the start that you are a bull in a china closet. We had a lot invested in that china closet, see. So we had to get you out of there."

I thought about it for a minute, then told him, "I take back what I said about you feds. Well, most of it. But it was a sloppy collar. How come one lone Chippy on a motorcycle, and how'd you even know I was there?"

Browning finished off the waffle and took a sip of coffee to wash it down before replying, in a very quiet voice, "Wasn't CHP, it was one of our special units hastily thrown into play. Couldn't risk getting the local constabulary involved but we wanted you in our hands. As for knowing you were there..."

"Yeah?"

"We had known where you were every minute of the day and night since that cute thing with Chase at the service station Sunday night."

I sighed, wished for a cigarette, and told him, "Yeah, you had me coming in. But you lost me, didn't you. The minute you got me into your hands, somebody tried to whack me off. I thought at first it was Gudgaloff. Now I'm not so sure. Who else would want me out of hand, Browning?"

"Call me this afternoon and we'll talk about it."

"I may not be alive this afternoon."

He sighed, told me, "Guess I'll have to risk that."

I said, "Thanks much. But I guess I don't want to. Why were you shadowing Tom Chase?"

He pushed his plate away and reached for his wallet. "Have to go, Joe. Early appointment."

"Why are you keeping him incommunicado?"

"I really have to go."

"What's your connection with Toni?"

He walked away and left me sitting there with little more than I'd come in with. Didn't even pay for my coffee.

Bull in a china closet, eh?

We'd see about that.

I dropped a buck on my ticket, handed it to the waitress, and returned immediately to the white frame cottage in Brentwood Park.

Bulls this guy hadn't seen yet.

CHAPTER
TWENTY

DON'T EVER rely on a remote-controlled garage door to protect your home against intruders. The operative devices are actually miniature radio transmitters and receivers. The commercially produced systems are limited to ten or twelve different radio channels at most, any of which can be keyed from any of the easily available remote control units that are carried in the car. You can buy a remote most anywhere for about twenty-five bucks and use it like a skeleton key; it will open any garage door, and at a pretty good distance. All you have to do is slide open the back panel and push the little switch along to find the radio channel that matches the receiver on the door.

That is the method I used to gain entry to the house in Brent-wood Park. I knew that the garage door was remotely operated

because I'd seen Browning close it from his car. All I had to do
was open the back of my unit and step along the channels while
holding the button down. Hit it on the third try from the middle
of the street and just pulled on in alongside another car as
though I belonged there.

Another tip: the door leading from the interior of the garage
into the house should be an "outside" door. This one was, but it
was framed for inside service. One kick and the whole thing fell
to the floor inside the house, framing and all.

It was the kitchen floor.

A guy was seated at the far wall with a telephone at his ear.
He was in shirtsleeves, wore a tie pulled loose at the neck and a
shoulder holster filled with heavy hardware. Took him about two
seconds to react to my crash-bang entrance, by then it was too
late to meet my charge with anything but the chin. He went out
like a light. I grabbed the phone and eased it to the floor without
a clatter, went on immediately to discover what was what but
already with a glimmer.

It was a "safe house," yeah, and I found Tom Chase just
emerging from a shower off one of the bedrooms.

He gawked at me and said, "Jesus, Joe!"

I returned to the kitchen without a word to my old pal,
checked out the guy in there. FBI, yeah. There should have
been at least one more in residence but I found no one else.

Tom was half-dressed when I returned for him. I grabbed the
rest of his outfit and said, "There's no time. Finish in the car."

He said, "No, you've got it wrong. I'm staying here."

I said, "Like hell you are," and I put his lights out too.

I carried him to the car and tucked him into the front seat,
threw his shoes and shirt inside, got the hell out of there quick.
All told I guess I was two minutes inside that house. Depending
on who was on the phone at the other end when I entered, I
figured maybe I got out with perhaps a minute to spare.

I took off west along surface streets, headed into Santa Monica, just wanting to get clear. Tom came out of it mad as hell and pouting before we'd gotten a mile away.

"Put your clothes on," I growled at him.

"Go to hell."

"That's where we're headed, pal. You can arrive half-dressed if you want to."

"This is crazy."

"For you, maybe, not for me. First sane moment I've had since Sunday night. Why'd you set me up, Tom?"

"You're crazy, I didn't set you up for anything."

"Sure you did. You set me up for Mathison, then you set me up for Putnam and Delancey. That took it off your back, didn't it. What kind of a deal did you cook with Browning?"

"You've got this all wrong, Joe."

"So lay it out for me."

"It started with Morris Putnam. He's my boss, you know."

"Was."

"Okay, was. His specialty was finance but he was basically CEO and General Manager for our division. Started going a little crazy several years back, I guess, but then it really got bad when George Delancey came over from the Pentagon. He was a contracts administrator for the Department of Defense. I found out that he'd been cozy with Putnam for years, feeding him inside information to cinch PowerTron's bids for fat defense contracts. Kickback scheme."

"And more than that."

"Well, yeah, after Delancey came to PowerTron. Between him and Putnam, they had the whole damned division locked into a network of ripoffs and kickbacks stretching from the Pentagon to subcontractors, I mean laterally and vertically. But they were working for themselves in that, not for the company. None of that money ever hit PowerTron's accounts."

"How'd you get onto it?"

"Pure accident. I spotted the two of them in a restaurant one night, wining and dining a guy I had just investigated as a possible subcontractor. The subcontract was awarded exactly two days later and I took a look at it. God, it was totally rigged."

"So what'd you do?"

"Nothing, at first. Didn't know where to take it, Joe. Didn't know who else might be involved. My loyalty is for the company, not for its Goddamned kinky executives. But here now I felt dirty myself. Just didn't know where to take it."

"So what'd you do with it?"

"Nothing. Just kept the eyes and ears open and waited for a chink. That finally came from the old man upstairs, Gordon Maxwell. He's Chairman and CEO of the entire company, offices back east."

"Uh-huh."

"We had a secret meeting, out here. He told me that he had it on reliable information that my division was in terrible trouble, under FBI investigation and maybe headed into a scandal strong enough to destroy the whole company, wanted to know what I knew about it."

"So you told him."

"Some . . . some. Still didn't know . . . well, I just didn't feel that I could trust any of them. I was scared, Joe, I don't mind admitting that. When it comes to the life or death of a multi-billion dollar corporation—maybe years in jail for these highpowered executives—well, the only rule is win. You know that. Men like that are capable of anything. So sure I was scared."

"What do you know about Toni Delancey?"

"Who?—oh, George's wife. Never met her."

"Why not?"

"She just never was around much, I guess. Why?"

"How 'bout Barbara Putnam?"

"She wasn't around much either, but I did see her at a few company functions. Very glamorous woman. But I don't know anything about her."

"Cherche LaFemme?"

"You've been hard at work, haven't you."

"Had to be. Tell me about Cherche."

Tom started getting into his shirt as he told me, "She operates a high-class brothel and call girl service, runs it like a club for millionaires. Some of our executives were involved."

"So?"

"So she is also involved with Nicholas Gudgaloff. And already I had begun to smell something more in all this than corporate crime. So I penetrated Lafemme's operation."

"Not very well," I sniffed.

"What?"

"Why'd you use your real name?"

He shrugged. "It just shook out that way. My entry was via a girl who already knew my name."

"Angélique?"

He gave me an irritated look. "Real name is Gina Terrabona. I recruited her. She cooked up a story to get me inside."

I just let it pass at that, for the moment, and instead asked him, "Why'd you try to call off the hit at the consulate?"

He said, "Gina was making headway with Gudgaloff. She was afraid that an overt action could blow everything up."

"It did," I said.

"Yeah," he agreed.

"Since then six people are dead and I've been charged with murder."

He said, "I'll square it, Joe."

"Sure you will. From your Goddamned safe house."

"Well . . . I'll do everything I can to . . ."

"What are you feeding Browning?"

"Cooperation, that's all."

"In return for . . . ?"

"Well, of course, to square myself."

"What about your *loyalty* to PowerTron?"

"Don't have that sorted out yet," he muttered.

"Lot of things you don't have sorted out," I informed him. "What happened to that fine police mental muscle you once had, pal? All gone into corporate flab?"

"Not entirely. Where are we going?"

I don't know why I said it, it just popped out of nowhere: "We're going to have a little talk with Frank Dostell."

It flipped him.

"Count me out," he said nervously. "I want no part of that guy. Stop the car. Let me out."

I said, "If I stop the car, Tom, it will be only to beat the shit out of you. You pulled me into this Goddamned mess, now you're going to help me find a way out of it. Why are you so afraid of Dostell?"

"Didn't say I was afraid of him," Tom growled. "Just want nothing to do with him."

"Too late," I said.

He said, "Dammit, Joe, I didn't know . . ."

"Didn't know what?"

"That it would ever come to this. Believe me, I'm sorry. I'll do what I can to square it."

"Start right now," I suggested. "What's the story on Mathison?"

Tom began putting his shoes on as he replied to that. "One of those rare birds, I guess—a kinky fed. You know the FBI has all these Russian offices under electronic surveillance all the time. It's a game that both powers play. All the phones are tapped and all radio communications are monitored. Occasionally the FBI gets a line on some guy who's trying to set up a sell for secret documents. Sometimes it's service personnel with access to classified training and maintenance manuals, sometimes it's people in industry with secrets to sell—and the jerks try to set it up by telephone."

"That's where people like Mathison come into it."

"Right. The FBI guy poses as a Russian agent and follows up on the contact. Classic sting operation, see. Then when the documents are actually passed, the jerk gets a handcuff in lieu of cash."

"Mathison was working a wrinkle on it."

"Yeah. He would position himself right in the middle, let the deal go through, share in the proceeds. Then I guess he got greedy, decided he wanted more than a share. Sometimes he would sting the jerk, make an arrest, copy the documents, then sell the copies. The jerk ended up in a prison cell and Mathison ended up with all the cash. If it couldn't be done tidily that way, the jerk might get dead suddenly and Mathison still got the cash."

"You know that for sure?—that last part?"

"Might be hard to prove in court... but, yeah, I know it for a fact, in at least two cases."

I said, "You've helped a little already, then. Feels a bit better to know what kind of guy I pulled a trigger on. How 'bout Browning? He's lily white?"

"Oh, he's lily white, yeah. Tough as nails but as square as they come."

"Why are they safing you?"

"They were nervous about uh..."

"About what?"

"Maybe they haven't uncovered all the bad apples. Mathison could have had conspirators in the ranks. They didn't want me found dead in a cell."

"You're that important to them?"

"I guess so."

"What about this Gina Terrabona? What's happening with her?"

"I don't know, Joe," he replied innocent-eyed.

"You've had no contact with her since Tuesday?"

"Browning picked me up on Tuesday. I've had no contact with anyone."

"You didn't see her about two o'clock this morning?"

"Don't be crazy. I told you, I've been in custody all this time."

"But you could have visitors."

"Hell no. They watch me like a hawk."

I gave him a hard look and said, "I talked to Miriam."

"Screw Miriam," was his response to that.

"Said she's contacted a lawyer to file for divorce."

"That's fine with me."

"You gave up your police career for that lady, pal."

He said, very quietly, "I gave up nothing for Miriam, Joe. Let's just leave her out of this."

"She called you a pervert."

He flinched, tried to cover it with a nervous laugh, asked, "What else did she call me?"

I replied, "I guess that covered it all."

"Didn't call me a junkie, huh?"

"No. Are you a junkie?"

"She probably thinks I am. We went to a couple of parties that turned out to be coke parties."

"But you don't use the stuff."

"You know me better than that."

"Yeah," I said agreeably. "But we still need to talk to Dostell."

That is where Tom Chase bailed out on me. He hit the lever and was rolling through the doorway before I could get a hand off the wheel.

I hit the brakes but I was only doing about twenty so I guess he had a tolerable enough landing. He was off the pavement and running by the time I could look back.

And that was the last time I saw my old pal Tom Chase alive.

CHAPTER
TWENTY-
ONE

SURE, I knew I'd done something really stupid. I'm not trying to alibi it when I say that I was simply playing the ear, taking it as it came, improvising as I went along. Hadn't known it was an FBI safe house when I went busting in there, had no particular plan in mind; from that point on, though, it was sheer stupidity.

Of course, I hadn't expected it to work out the way it did, either. I'd been wanting a crack at Tom Chase for a couple of days, thinking he could fill in some gaps for me. When I saw him standing there in that bedroom in Brentwood Park, it was like instant gratification and I simply seized the moment. Meant to take him back after we'd had our talk.

But now I was really into it.

What I had done, in essence, was to break a prisoner out of federal detention.

In a larger sense, I had kidnapped a prisoner from protective custody and exposed him to the very danger from which he was being protected. I had also assaulted a federal agent and interfered with due process.

I was sure that Browning would be able to think of several other charges, if those were not enough to inspire the judge to revoke my bail and maybe even order it forfeited. So I was not worried only for myself. I had to think about Cherche, too, and where a forfeiture would leave her.

So yeah, I was kicking my own ass up and down the streets as I cruised around hoping to find Tom Chase and take him back to where he belonged. Maybe then Browning would not be mad enough to throw the book at me.

But I did not find even a sniff of Tom, not until it was too late. I'd been cruising for fifteen minutes, back and forth across the area, and had decided to give it up when I spotted a crowd of people and the telltale red and blue flashers of a police cruiser at the next intersection. This was on Santa Monica Boulevard just outside the L.A. city limits, at a small cross street. The crowd was gathered outside a smoke shop at the corner. A patrolman was trying to handle the crowd. I could hear sirens approaching in the distance, and I had that sinking feeling in the gut that I already knew what was attracting that crowd.

I double-parked behind the cruiser and joined the onlookers, pushed my way inside. The gut had known, yeah. Tom Chase lay there oozing blood from about forty holes. An ambulance screamed in with several more police cars in tow. But it was all over, pal. It was all over. And it was my damned fault.

They talk about a guy's life flashing in front of his eyes as he's about to die. That happened to me, standing there in that crowd over my old pal's body, but it wasn't my life that flashed, it was his, and ours together. That flash contained all the lousy patrols and stake-outs, shoot-outs, drinking bouts, locker room jokes, the good times and the bad times, the dreams and the fears of two young cops on mean streets together. It was all there in a single flash, yeah, and I wanted to just sit down on the God-damned curb and cry.

But there was no place on the curb to sit and I guess I never learned how to cry like a man in public. The cops had arrived in force, too, and were taking control of the situation. I allowed myself to be shoved back against the front of the smoke shop and I just stood there for a couple of minutes, too stunned and stupid to think or act, but then my policeman's brain began to assert itself as I overheard one of the cops talking to a witness.

It was the proprietor of the smoke shop, an old man with excitement in the voice, and apparently he'd seen it all and more. "He come busting in just as I was opening the shop. He was all out of breath, panting like he'd been running a long way, wanted to use the telephone. Flashed a badge, see, and grabbed the telephone. Talked to someone for just a second, didn't say more than three words—just gave the corner here, I think—then went to stand just inside the door, watching the street. Stood there for about five minutes and I was getting damn nervous about it. I didn't really see that badge good. Any jerk can buy a badge. But then this car came along and I guess he saw it coming. He turned and waved at me and said thanks, and went out to meet the car at the curb. They shot him from the car as he was walking toward it. They shot him with a machine gun from the car. Was he really a policeman?"

Had been, yeah, a long time ago...damned good policeman.

I had to get away from there. Anywhere, just away. So I went away. And had a good cry in private. I think it was for both of us, Tom and me.

I CALLED Browning and broke the news to him myself. Took a while to reach him. He was out of the office but they relayed the call via mobile service and I caught him in his car. He said not a word in reaction for a good ten seconds, then all he said was, "Well that's beautiful, just beautiful."

I said, "Yeah."

He asked me, in a curiously controlled voice, "What time did you lift him out of there, Joe?"

"From the safe house? It was about ten minutes after you left me. Why?"

I guess he'd been reading the emotion in my voice, because he said to me, "Don't beat yourself up over this. You didn't shorten his life any. You extended it."

"What do you mean?" I asked.

"Where are you now?"

"I'm in Santa Monica. What do you mean by—?"

"I'm at the safe house. Come on back."

I was thinking about it when he broke the silence to say, "It's okay. Come on over. Want you to see this."

"Okay," I replied. "I'm about fifteen minutes away."

"I'll be here," he assured me.

I couldn't figure it. Just couldn't figure it. But I drove back to Brentwood Park. And then, yeah, I stopped beating up on myself just a little.

I COULD not get within two blocks of the place by car. Streets were filled with firefighting equipment and a lot of hell was still going down, throughout that neighborhood. Browning must have passed the word to admit me through the periphery containment because I was passed right on through on my name alone.

It had appeared from a distance that the entire neighborhood was on fire but it turned out to be only three houses involved in addition to the safe house, and the firemen had knocked down the blaze in all but one when I arrived.

There was a black hole in the ground where the safe house had been. Charred rubble was flung all over the area. I found Browning talking to a fire captain. He excused himself and came over to join me while I just stood there gaping at that hole in the ground.

"Looks nuked," I commented.

"Had to be a hell of a charge," the fed agreed. "Someone really wanted it to blow."

"When did it happen?"

"It blew at seven o'clock. That must be very close to the time you were here."

I asked him, "What time did you leave the restaurant?"

"It was six-forty."

"Very close, yeah," I said. "I came straight back here, so that's about six forty-five. I wasn't here five minutes. But close enough, for sure." A thought hit me, so I expressed it. "One of your agents was here when I left. He was unconscious. Have you found . . . ?"

"We've found nothing yet. Just one agent?"

I said, "Just one, yeah."

"You're sure?"

"I'm sure. Guy about average height, thirty-ish, brown curly hair, wore a big six-shooter in shoulder harness."

Browning said, "Uh-huh. Only one?"

I said it again. "Only one, yeah."

He sighed deeply and said, "Let's get away from here."

The fed gave me a ride to my car, then I followed him to the same restaurant where we'd talked before. We had coffee and talked some more. He turned out to be an okay guy, it seemed. The barriers of officialdom were down and we just talked like men. I explained how I had blundered into the safe house looking for anything and nothing, how surprised I'd been to find Tom there, and why I took him out of there. And I gave it to him straight, the gist of the whole dialogue with Tom, the curious bit about Frank Dostell, Tom's dash from the car and my attempt to get him back.

Browning did not act surprised at any of it.

When I told him about the shooting in Santa Monica, he just nodded and said, "That's twice. I'll alert the Santa Monica police to check for a ballistics match with the freeway shooting. That could prove interesting."

I asked him, "What kind of gun was it, the freeway hit?"

"Uzi," he replied pithily.

"Well, that narrows it down. There are only about a million of those in this town."

"We need only one," he said.

I liked the way he said "we," so I told him, "I feel like a jerk about all this, Browning, but I'll try to set it right. What can I do to make your job easier?"

"You can go back to jail," he said soberly.

"Other than that," I said.

"Just keep doing what you're doing."

"Yeah?"

"Yeah. But I won't have it on my conscience."

"Meaning?"

"Meaning you are a lightning rod, Joe. You'll likely end up in a grave beside your friend, Chase. But while you're with us, things do happen. I'm content for now to watch it happen."

"Like that, eh?"

"Exactly like that."

"You won't revoke my bail."

He sighed. "No. I should. And I should throw your key away. That would be doing you a favor. But I'm all out of favors for a while." He stood up, picked up both tickets, said, "The coffee is on me, but don't try to make it a habit."

"Will you be taking a look at Tom now?"

"Yes. Want to tag along?"

I waved it off, said, "Thanks. I already did my requiem."

"Whose china closet?" he asked lightly, "are you contemplating now?"

"Maybe my own," I replied.

"Your own?"

I nodded my head, offering no further explanation.

The fed said, "Don't get too wild," and walked away.

I think all the "wild" had left me, at that point.

That, I could understand.

But I wasn't sure I understood why Special Agent Browning was being so damned nice to me.

Unless, of course, I could simply take him at his word and he was not being nice in the deeper sense.

Or unless he had blown up his own safe house.

CHAPTER
TWENTY-
TWO

TWO LARGE inconsistencies were gnawing at me as I went back to Beverly Hills that morning, one squarely in the front of the head and the other somewhat buried in the twisting memory of those past twenty-four hours.

The one up front had to do with Toni.

And it had to do with Nicky.

They'd been together, went to Malibu to find Frank Dostell. Shortly thereafter, according to Nicky's version of the events, Toni asked him to drop her at a house in Brentwood Park. He told me that she appeared to "admit herself." He watched her go inside, then he left. A couple of hours later, Toni shows up in Beverly Hills bleeding from a beating at unknown hands.

So far, okay.

I had been focussed by rage, intent on discovering what actually happened to Toni, and I'd been inclined to take things at face value.

But then that whole thing falls apart when that house in Brentwood Park is revealed as an FBI safe house. A safe house is a sort of secret jail where the feds keep important witnesses who could drop dead before telling their stories to judge and jury. It is all strictly legal under the Federal Witness Protection Act but it is carried out under great secrecy and with extraordinary precautions.

So how the hell could Toni have known about the house in Brentwood Park?

And if she had known about it—which would seem to suggest some tie-in with the FBI—why would she then endanger it by asking an agent of the KGB to take her there?

See?—it made no sense.

On the other hand, Nicky himself had sent *me* there. If not via Toni, then how had he known about it? And if he'd known that it was a safe house, why did he tip his hand by sending me there?

Made no sense.

Unless...

Unless, of course, he'd known that the joint was wired to blow at seven o'clock and he'd hoped to include me in those festivities.

That brings up something else, see.

I had told Browning during our first tête-à-tête that Nicky told me that he'd dropped Toni at Browning's house at two o'clock. At the moment, of course, I was assuming that the Brentwood Park address was where Browning lived. But Browning should have tumbled right away that I was talking about the Brentwood house, that I'd staked it out and followed him from there—otherwise how could I be sitting there talking to him over breakfast in a restaurant five minutes away?

But I got no rise from Browning over that info. I was telling him in essence that both Nicky and Toni had been outside that safe house a few short hours earlier. Why didn't that trouble him? Maybe it had—but if it had, he was damned good at covering his feelings—and why hadn't he moved immediately to safeguard his prisoner? If that had been me, I would have had a flying squad over there and moving that prisoner in the wink of an eye.

Why hadn't Browning done that?

See?—there were these troubling inconsistencies.

The other began working its way clear of the gray matter while I was mulling those.

The other had to do with Browning also.

So I called my friend at LAPD and checked it out.

I asked him, "Were you able to get any good ballistics evidence on that freeway shooting?"

He wasn't exactly friendly but not hostile either, had to go look it up, came back to tell me, "We got some pretty good ones, yeah, very little deformation. Steel-jacketed hardpoints, nine millimeter."

"Any conclusions as to the type of weapon that fired them?"

"You know better than that, Joe."

I knew better than that, yeah.

But when I'd asked Browning about it, he came right back with, "Uzi."

Of course he could have put it together as an educated guess, but it hadn't come out that way and I couldn't figure Browning as a sloppy thinker. The Uzi is not the only nine millimeter submachine gun. But it had just popped out: "Uzi."

It was a bother, yeah.

I still could not distinguish friend from foe.

THE OLD mansion was quiet and sleepy at ten A.M. The maid buzzed me through and met me at the front door, took me through to the pool area, parked me at a patio table and quickly produced Danish, orange juice, and a silver pot of coffee.

I hadn't touched any of that except for an experimental sip of orange juice when the "secretary," the tall blonde identified as Alexandra, came out to greet me. She was dressed for aerobics, legwarmers and the whole bit, and a large white towel was draped about her shoulders. Makeup she did not need, and none was in evidence as she dropped gracefully onto a chair opposite me and dazzled me with a smile.

"You're early," she informed me. "This is like the middle of the night for most of us here."

"But not you."

"We try to stagger the hours so that someone is always around and alert. I am usually in bed by two A.M., so I'm up earlier too." She was blotting herself with the towel, showed me a sort of embarrassed smile, apologized for her sweat. "I try to start my day with a good workout and I usually take a swim to cool down. Join me?"

I said, "Thanks, no. I already had my cooldown. When does the rest of the household begin to stir?"

"Never before noon. Usually about two. Cherche for sure is good for two."

"Did you hear about the excitement last night?"

"We have excitement every night," she said with a smile. "Was there something out of the ordinary?"

"Maybe not," I replied.

I suddenly felt very tired. It was Friday, and the weight of the week was bearing down on me. I'd been chased by dogs, seduced, kidnapped, shot at, set up, set down, booked on murder charges, jailed, played with by the FBI, the KGB, maybe the CIA and God knew who else; I'd been wooed, betrayed, misled, tricked—and I'd seen an old friend die. Through it all I had slept maybe eight hours, had eaten hardly anything, and had smoked not a single damned cigarette.

Now this gorgeous blonde who could make a fortune posing for cameras was sitting two feet away in the dazzling sunshine and taking off her clothes with a smile right before my eyes and inviting me to join her in the pool.

I felt two hundred and sixty years old and incapable of even toddling over to that pool, let alone frolicking in it with a nude bunny—yet that stupid, blind, unreasoning male part of me that responds to such stimuli was responding as usual.

She was saying, "This could be a good day, Joe, until two o'clock," and she was skinning the tights down from the shoulders, twisting and turning in the chair to get free of them, with only now and then coverage from the towel.

I said, "It's a terrible day, Alex. I just saw a friend off to the morgue."

"All the more reason to lighten up," she told me, free and clear now and coming off the chair.

I had to close my eyes to shut that out. I heard her giggle in a very ladylike way, then I heard the splash as she entered the pool.

Closing the eyes had been a mistake.

They did not want to open again, and I drifted in a kind of twilight sleep full of lazy hallucinations while remaining vaguely aware of my physical surroundings. I knew when Alexandra returned to the table but I did not see her, and I heard female voices in quiet discussion without comprehending the words.

Some time later I knew that I was on my feet and moving with assistance, and then someone was undressing me and putting me to bed, but the reality of the physical world was confused and lost in the swirling fogs of a waning consciousness and I was powerless to bring the focus in. So I merely surrendered to it. I remember thinking that maybe death was something like this. I think maybe I even confused the experience with death and, funny thing, I didn't even mind.

I WAS never one for nightmares but I guess I came as close to one as I'd ever be during that brief sleep. I dreamed that I was in hell. Satan was taunting me with still-frame scenes from my life on earth—but they were not bad scenes, they were good ones. My hands were tied over my head and I was suspended by a rope in a big wooden vat bubbling with decomposing excrement and vile sewage. I was up to my chin in it. Tom Chase came floating by and he looked at me pleadingly but I couldn't make a move toward him. Toni was there somewhere with her banged up face but I could never get a clear look at her as she bobbed around with the bubbles surrounding her. There were other faces in that mess, too, but I recognized none of them. Meanwhile Satan is showing me all these happy scenes and telling me what I jerk I'd been all my life. Once, there, he looked just like Nicky—another time like Browning—but the faces kept changing off and I knew that Satan was very confused about his own identity.

It was a very long dream and totally confused. Somewhere near the end I'd managed to pull my feet up out of the muck and I was trying to kick ol' Satan into it. I finally connected with a good one to his chin, but he was Ivan now, and that's where I woke up.

I was in a gorgeous room with sunlight streaming through the window, lying in a tangle of covers atop a very nice bed that smelled of roses and felt like velvet to my naked body. Alexandra stepped out of a connecting bathroom and gave me a curious look. She was wearing a sheer negligee and nothing but.

"Are you fully awake this time?" she asked me.

"Which time is this?" I asked back with an uncooperative voice.

"It's nearly two o'clock," she told me. "You've been dead to the world for about four hours, passed out on the patio. Do you remember talking to me beside the pool?"

I said, "Sure. Did you enjoy your swim?"

"Too short," she replied, wrinkling her nose for effect. "You must weigh three hundred pounds. Thought we'd never get you up the stairs."

"Whose bed is this?"

"Mine."

"Did we have fun?"

She laughed. "Maybe you did. I think you were wrestling bears the whole time. Look, I have to get dressed. But you're welcome to use the shower any time you're ready. And please shave."

I felt my face and agreed, "Yeah, I've got some stubble here. Is this still Friday?"

She laughed again and said, "Of course. And that is more than mere stubble, my friend. You're like sandpaper."

"Checked it out, eh?"

She lightly replied, "Remember what I told you last night?"

I said, "Yeah, and you told me at the pool that this was a very good day. Talk dirty to me."

She just laughed and went back into the bathroom.

I fought my way clear of the tangled covers and got both feet on the floor. That was quite a victory, but I was beginning to feel alive again and to feel glad about that.

Alexandra reached back and patted my belly as I squeezed past her en route to the shower. "Leave something for me," she suggested playfully. "But you'll have to put it on hold. I'm at work in ten minutes. Have to arrange a special party for Mr. Woodman."

I turned back from the shower door to say, "It will keep. Who is Woodman?"

"One of Cherche's very special accounts. And the guest list is huge."

Cherche's special parties were not at the top of my interest at the moment. "How's Angélique?" I asked.

"You'll have to hold forever for her," she replied, still playing. "Angélique quit today."

"Quit?"

"Yes. Packed up and left early this morning."

"The damned bubbles," I said, recalling the dream.

"What?"

"Private joke, I muttered, and stepped into the shower.

But it was no joke.

And neither were the bubbles.

I needed to get dressed and out of there damned quick. I don't know about the significance of dreams. But I knew for damned sure that Toni Delancey was in deep trouble and probably getting deeper with every passing hour. I'd already dreamed away four precious hours. Now it was time to start bursting bubbles.

CHAPTER
TWENTY-
THREE

IT WOULD be at least another hour before Cherche would be presenting herself to the new day, so I left her a note and promised to report back at the earliest opportunity, got out of there at just a little past two o'clock.

Needed to look some people up, needed to do it quickly and efficiently, because I knew that time was running out and there was a long way to go—like a two-minute drill in football, starting at your own ten yard line. Problem with that allegory is that there were no yard markers and no chalk marks to show where I was actually starting from, and the stadium clock was out of order. I could've been starting from the one foot mark with only one second on the official clock.

I knew that I had to get out there and hustle, just the same, and try to make something happen. So if dreams have any meaning beyond their moment, I needed to go crashing through the bubbles of this very real cesspool and drag Toni onto the grass where I could look at her with a clear focus. If I am mixing my metaphors, so be it—I'm sure you get my meaning, even if I was a bit unsure of it myself at the time.

It had occurred to me that several common threads were holding this entire weave together. One of those threads was marked *PowerTron*—and now the three top West Coast executives of the company were dead by violence. Those three shared other things in common, as well.

Chase's widow, Miriam, had referred to her disgraced husband as a pervert and apparently she'd been shocked and appalled, in that connection, by some objects that had been found in his car when he was arrested—enough so that she had been planning a divorce when he was killed.

Cherche had told me that Putnam and Delancey, also, had exhibited sexual problems that disqualified them from membership in her exclusive sex club. Toni was Delancey's widow and she had sadly left him some time earlier. Barbara was Putnam's widow and apparently she had been "partying" at a distant resort while he lay dead in his own home.

So what else tied these guys together in death? Criminal greed? Treason? Drug addiction? If at least two out of three of those, was that begging a coincidence or what?—that all three were top executives of the same company, all three were mixed up in a deadly game, all three had succumbed to that game?

I had to know.

The telephone at the Delancey home rang twenty times and no one answered.

Next on my list was the Chase home. The phone got picked up there on the third ring and Miriam's mopey voice made me wish I could have skipped that one. I said, "This is Joe. Have you heard?"

I guess she'd been crying and the voice was still foggy. "Yes. I heard."

"Can I come over?"

"It isn't necessary."

"I said nothing about necessary. Can I?"

She thought about it for about five seconds before replying, "Okay," and hung up.

So I went to see Miriam. Stopped off first at my safety deposit box and retrieved the five-thousand "retainer" from her husband, took it with me.

It was strained and stiff there. I think I've told you that we had never been friends, exactly. I gave her the five grand and told her, "Tom left this with me for safekeeping."

"Where did he steal it?" she asked in a voice going very bitter very quickly.

"He didn't say. Maybe he'd been saving it for a rainy day."

"It has been nothing but rainy days all this year," she said. "My lawyer discovered that he had gone through everything. We're broke." She amended that with a twisted smile. "*I'm* broke. He even borrowed to the maximum on his insurance policies. We owe every bank and loan company in town. I called PowerTron today, after...he'd cashed in all his company stock and borrowed against his deferred compensation. Dammit, Joe, all that was half mine! He had no right!"

"He was in trouble, Miriam," I said as gently as I could.

"Oh boy, was he in trouble! The trunk of his car was stuffed with leather corsets and whips and all that crazy stuff! How could he have *spent* all that money? My lawyer says it will be impossible to trace it if he put it in secret bank accounts overseas."

"Save the effort," I suggested. "I think he spent it. I think I know how and I think I know where."

"Do you use the same whores?"

I kept it as genteel as possible. Miriam was hurting, I knew that. And although maybe she had been partly responsible for all that herself, it was no time for anything but consolation. "He didn't spend it that way, Miriam. I believe he was an addict."

She said, "Oh! God!"

"Ring a bell somewhere?"

"About six months ago..."

"Yeah?"

"Well there was this raunchy crowd in Malibu that he was trying to run with. Dragged me to several of the parties. I just couldn't handle it. Told him to leave me out of any future plans with that bunch. I believe they were using cocaine. They smoked pot, too, I know that for sure. Place reeked of it."

"Remember any names?"

"No, I..."

"Does the name Dostell ring any bells?"

I saw the light appear in her brain. She said, "That was one."

"One of the beach duplexes right off the highway?"

"Yes. They skinny-dipped in the surf by moonlight."

I sighed and told her, "Well let that be his epitaph. It's probably as kind a one as you're going to find." I turned to go, paused at the door to tell her, "Look into his police pension rights. There could be something there."

"Thanks," she said brightly. "I'll do that. Thanks for bringing the money and... thanks for coming, Joe. I really do feel better."

I was sure she did. As deadly as it may be, a cocaine addiction is an easier rival to contemplate than chains and whips—more understandable somehow—but really the two were the same.

Both spelled compulsive behavior and a monkey on the back for sure.

Myself, I felt not a damned bit better.

THE DRIVE of the Putnam home in Altadena was jammed with cars. The front door stood open and it was almost a party atmosphere inside. Well-dressed people were standing about with drinks in hand and talking spiritedly, laughter here and there, trays of fingerfoods being passed around.

It was a wake for Morris Putnam.

A pretty woman of indeterminate years came over to greet me. "You must be Joe."

"And that makes you Mary." I'd spoken to her again by telephone just a few minutes earlier.

Turns out that she is Barbara Putnam's sister. She gave me a conspiratorial hug and looked quickly around as though searching for a face in the crowd, told me, "Barb is about somewhere."

"Never mind," I said. "We'll cross eventually."

She replied. "Oh good, meanwhile I'll just keep you to myself. Cocktail?"

We walked to a makeshift stand-up bar where a middleaged man was acting as bartender. I took a rock and a splash of bourbon and we went on out to the yard where some smokers were gathered in exile. I asked Mary, "How's she taking it?"

"Surprisingly, Joe, she's taking it pretty bad."

"Why surprisingly?"

"Well...it's no secret that..."

"What?"

She laughed with a trace of embarrassment and replied,

"Don't speak ill of the dead but things have not been exactly cozy around here for quite a while. I assumed you knew. Barb would have been gone long ago except for the children. Hell, I don't care, I'm going to speak ill. He was a son of a bitch and I'm glad my sister is finally free of that man."

I tasted my booze and said, "No, I hadn't known."

"Consider yourself educated."

I smiled. "There are always two sides, aren't there?"

"Hey, whose side are you on? Let's see, two sides..." She had her face screwed into a comical grimace. "...nope, I find only one. Cheer up, Joe. If you came to eulogize Morris, you're going to be in a company of one. Speaking of which, his own company has disavowed him. Barb just learned that they fired him the day he died."

I said, "No!"

"Yep. Locked his office and sealed up all his records. I just know there's going to be a scandal. I feel bad about that for the kids, but... well, if it will help Barb erase this man from her life... am I presuming too much?—or could I suggest—"

I had to head it off. This lady was a compulsive talker and romantic, and I'd given her a bit too much encouragement. Didn't want her to end up feeling like a total fool, so I told her, "You've got it wrong, Mary. I barely know Barbara. In fact—I'll level with you—don't know her at all. I'm a cop."

She drew back to give me a whole new kind of scrutiny, wavering between a smile and a frown, finally said to me, "How exciting. I've never met a detective."

"Now you have."

"So you are investigating...?"

I said, "Follow up. Routine, actually. Just trying to put some background together."

"But you have found the killer. The man you arrested..."

"It's pretty well nailed down, yes."

"So... what do you need to know?"

"Why Morris was killed."

"Oh! Well it had something to do with business, didn't it."

"Monkey business, maybe," I replied with a wink.

She said, "Aha, okay. Then you're on the right track. There was an unnatural relationship with George Delancey, we knew that. So maybe it was a homosexual triangle."

I told her, "That's a possibility, of course. I'm also looking into the drug angle."

"Oh! Yes! Right!"

"You knew about his addiction, then?"

"Well, no. Not exactly. But he'd been acting very strangely. That could be it."

I drew her farther aside and lowered my voice to a conspiratorial murmur. "Can I depend on you to keep something under your hat for a while, Mary?"

"Oh! Absolutely!"

"Morris had been involved in a sex club. I feel that he also could have been a cocaine addict. Delancey was involved in all that too. I am trying to determine if another man was involved. His name is Tom Chase. He was the security chief for Power-Tron. Have you heard the name?"

Her eyes were as big as saucers. She said, "Oh my God," in an awed voice.

"You know him?"

She shook her head. "No. But what kind of sex club?"

"Do me a favor," I quietly requested. "Go find Barbara. Get a moment alone with her. Ask her if she knows Tom Chase."

I had just made that lady's day. She was almost staggering with excitement as she hurried back into the house.

Maybe it was not the kindest addition to a wake.

But I got the information I wanted.

Putnam and Chase had been close friends, on and off the job.

There had been some connection in the past, prior to Tom's employment by PowerTron, and Putnam himself had brought him into the company.

But there had been a "falling out" recently.

Just two weeks before the tragedy, there had been a violent argument between the two men in Putnam's study, and Chase had been "thrown out."

And Putnam had commanded his wife: "Never let that man in this house again!"

The bubbles were beginning to burst, yes.

And the odor was awful.

CHAPTER
TWENTY-FOUR

I WENT out to PowerTron and walked into the central security offices at a few minutes before five. There was a late Friday afternoon atmosphere in there, line of unoccupied desks, one woman working at a file cabinet and another tidying the counter area. The one at the counter flicked her eyes at the wall clock as she gave me about ten percent of her attention and went on with her tidying. I asked for Tom Chase and that got me maybe ninety percent.

"Mr. Chase was terminated on Wednesday," she informed me.

That came as no great shock. I was prepared for it, in fact, in one form or another. I flashed my ID and told the clerk, "I need to see his successor, then. Tell him it's an FBI matter."

Her eyes flicked to the clock again as though to confirm the number of minutes remaining before her week was ended. "Mr.

Hightower is Acting Chief. Just a minute, I'll see..."

She retreated to a line of private offices at the rear, said something into an open doorway, and kept on going. The other woman followed quickly behind her and I saw neither of them again. A man came out of the office immediately and approached me with a set smile which rapidly evaporated as he drew closer.

This was the guy who two days earlier had led me to Altadena and the cold corpses of Morris Putnam and George Delancey. Several small circular bandaids on the forehead concealed the minor damage he had sustained in our first meeting.

I said, "We need to talk, Hightower."

Took him a couple of seconds to make up his mind on that issue. Then he said, "Come on back," and buzzed me through the security door.

We went into his private office, sat down, went right to work. "What do you want, Copp?"

"Were you Acting Chief the last time we met?"

"Yes."

"So all that razzmatazz about moonlighting—"

"Wasn't razzmatazz. I wasn't acting in an official capacity."

"Uh-huh. So who appointed you?"

"What do you mean?"

"You told me you were working directly for Putnam."

"That was a lie."

I said, "One of many, eh? So who was giving you orders?"

"That's none of your concern."

"The hell it isn't. You knew I would follow you from the restaurant, didn't you."

"Don't know what you mean."

"Sure you do. Someone wanted to place me at the murder scene. You led me up there. Tell me why."

"No, you have it wrong. Maybe you have an overbloated sense

of your own importance. Maybe you weren't the target."

"You think maybe you were?"

He nodded. "Seemed that way."

"That why you split without phoning it in?"

"Would you have phoned it in, Copp?"

I said, "Maybe not. Are you telling me that someone sent you up there?"

"Telling you nothing. Why'd you go back? That was dumb."

"I hadn't been there."

"Your gun had been there."

"Not attached to me. I think you know that. I think you iced those people, Hightower. Then you sucked me up there to take the fall."

He showed me a sober smile. "Why would I do that?"

"Why would someone make you Acting Chief?"

"The ex-Chief was behind bars. I was next in line. Simple as that."

"But you had all this moonlight work in the meantime, this special assignment. Who was punching your ticket for that, if not Putnam?"

"That isn't in your need to know."

"I'm putting it there."

"Go to hell, then. The interview is over." He picked up the telephone and dangled it casually by the left hand. "Start a ruckus in here, Copp, and I'll bury your ass in company cops. Aren't you out on bail?"

I placed a foot on the edge of his desk and straightened the leg. The heavy desk slid forward, jammed his swivel chair into the well and pinned him to the wall. I slapped the phone out of his hand and pulled the plug on it.

"Difference between you and me," I told him, "is that you're trying to succeed and I'm just trying to survive. Means nothing to threaten me with minor inconveniences when the hounds of hell are tearing at my flesh. The interview is over when I say it's over."

This man was not good at bearing pain.

He weakly gasped, "Let off. You're crushing me."

"So now you know how it feels," I said. "Someone is crushing me too. Who appointed you Acting Chief?"

"Putnam did, before he died."

"Before someone helped him die," I corrected him. "That happened early Wednesday. Chase was arrested late Tuesday. So when did you know about this wonderful change in your status?"

"Last weekend," Hightower groaned.

"So Tom knew even before Tuesday that he was out of a job."

"I don't know if he knew."

"He might have guessed?"

"Well I'm sure he knew that something was brewing."

"How would he know that?"

"Putnam was very unhappy with him."

"A personal matter, though, not job-related."

"Both, I think. Things had not been going well for Tom for some time."

"Were you friends with him?"

"Not exactly."

"How would you rate his job performance?"

"Excellent."

"So why would he have a job-related problem?"

"If the CEO distrusts you, I'd say that's job-related."

"Did Putnam tell you that he distrusted Tom?"

"Not in so many words, but..."

"He told you last weekend that he was firing him."

"Yeah."

"How did he put it to you?"

"Just told me to get ready to take over. Told me I shouldn't let Tom take any records out of the plant."

"He didn't tell you when you'd be taking over?"

"I just knew that it would be soon."

"What do you suppose he was waiting for?"

"He didn't say and I didn't ask."

"What kind of records?"

"What?"

"He said you should not let Tom take any records."

"I don't know what he meant by that."

"Guess."

"There were rumors of a GSA audit. I don't know."

"What would an audit like that entail?"

"Just, I guess, looking into the costs and the billings and all that."

"Tom wouldn't have access to those records, would he?"

"The classified stuff, sure. That's a big part of our job here in security, running herd on classified documents."

"Come on, they don't classify the financial stuff."

"Sometimes, yeah, we have to, when the costs are tied to research and development, secret specifications and the like. 'Course the billings just recap all that by reference. But sometimes the detail stuff is classified."

I said, "Why would Tom want to take stuff like that out of the plant?"

"I don't know. You said guess. I was guessing."

"Tom knew he was about to be fired."

"Yes."

"Did he talk to you about it?"

"No."

"What about the sex parties?"

Hightower blinked and replied, "What about them?"

"Did you ever attend any?"

"No."

"You were never invited?"

"No."

I smiled. "Would you go?"

He smiled back, despite the pressure on his rib cage. "I might. Depends."

"Even if that is what got Tom in all the trouble?"

The smile faded. "I don't think that was it."

"Putnam is dead."

"Yes."

"Delancey is dead."

"Uh-huh."

"Now Chase is dead. Who's next?"

Hightower strained ineffectually against the desk as he replied, "Isn't that enough?"

"Depends on your point of view," I told him. "Looks to me like someone is trying to blot something out. Who would need to do that?"

"Beats me."

I kicked the desk a bit tighter and held it there. "Think hard."

The eyes were beginning to bulge. "I swear I don't know anything about it!"

So maybe he didn't.

I let the pressure off and told him, "I have it from an impeccable source that Morris Putnam was fired Wednesday morning before he died, that his office was locked and a seal put on his personal records. Did you know about that?"

"Yes, I knew about it. I handled the security angle."

"Oh whose orders?"

"I was called personally by General Maxwell himself. He's the Chairman and CEO back east."

"What'd he tell you?"

"He just said that Putnam should be barred from entering the premises."

"Didn't tell you why?"

"Just that Putnam was out and should be kept out."

"Why do you think he was fired?"

"I don't know."

"Was Delancey fired too?"

"Yes."

"And barred from the premises?"

"Yes."

"What do you think is happening with PowerTron?"

"God, I don't know," he replied.

I said, "If I were wearing your hat right now, pal, I think I'd be giving it some thought."

"I'll do that. Thanks."

"And sleeping with one eye open."

"You think I'm in danger?"

"Do you think you're not?" I asked, and left him on that note.

A "theory of the case" had begun to form for me during that interrogation. That means the broad overview, with all the seemingly disparate pieces falling into a pattern of cause and effect.

I didn't have all the causes in total focus yet, and certainly not all of the effects, but I felt for the first time some coherent sense of flow that I could throw a saddle on and ride into the dirt.

I would have to do that, I knew.

Or I would die.

CHAPTER
TWENTY-FIVE

IT WAS nearing onto dusk when I hit the Delancey place, an upscale hillside home worth maybe half a mil in today's market —not quite as grand as the Putnam digs but close. I entered through a rear window, found the atmosphere in there not exactly pleasant because the house had been shut up tight for a long time, it seemed. The windows were all heavily draped and the air conditioning system was shut down.

Very stylish place, though, with a circular stairway lifting to a loft room and bedrooms beyond, a large he and she bath complete with Jacuzzi and wardrobes connecting separate master sleeperies, one very austere and the other femininely sensual— male clothing in one, female in the other. They had not routinely slept together. For some reason I took comfort in that—I guess because it seemed more like an arrangement than a marriage, but it was a sad thought too.

Two large suitcases stood open atop her bed and articles of clothing had been rather carelessly packed into them. That morning's newspaper lay folded on the foot of the bed. I found bloodstained puffs of cotton and an open bottle of hydrogen peroxide in the bathroom, evidence that someone had recently been cleaning minor wounds.

She'd been there, all right, at some time during that day. I recalled the telephone conversation when she thought I was the coroner and she told me that she needed her husband's body released because she was leaving town—"leaving for Europe," I think she said.

But had she already left, deciding to not bother with the big suitcases?

I poked around for a while up there but found no clues to her actual intentions—felt a bit peculiar going through her personal things—finally gave it up and went back downstairs for a quick check of those premises. Mail was stacked on a table in the entry hall, all of it addressed to George, all bills and advertisements—too late, folks, he's gone and left no forwarding address. The finality of that struck me in a way I'd never thought of death before. I vaguely wondered what George had worried about and dreamed about—what he feared the most and loved the most—and how it all reduced to exactly nothing now that there were no more tomorrows.

In the kitchen I found pungent coffee simmering in a Silex, a cereal bowl and a spoon rinsed and resting in a dish drainer, bare refrigerator and a nearly bare cupboard. I turned off the Silex, in case no one would be around to do so later.

This home had recently been nothing but a headquarters, maybe not even that. Obviously George had spent very little time here since the separation. Now these few meager tracings of habitation only emphasized the neglect and made poignant the shattered hopes with which this home must have been established. I'd never seen the man in life but I'd seen him in cold, stiff death, an inanimate caricature of a human being—and I grieved a little for George Delancey in his barren kitchen. Okay, I grieved for Toni too—and I would have put those two together again if I could.

But all the king's horses and men could not have done that even a week earlier, and I saw why when I found the little den behind the study. It was only about an eight-by-ten cubicle without windows, and it contained only a bigscreen projection-type TV with VCR, an overstuffed chair, a small table. Plus a video library with about fifty cassettes of the X variety— double and triple X, maybe, if you consider the genres of porn. This was all lash and leather culture, pure S&M, not a good recipe for marital health if it turns one on and the other off.

I went out the way I'd come in, found a neighbor grunting over a buried lawn sprinkler in the adjacent yard, a silver-haired oldster who'd probably spotted me coming in and whose curiosity was lying in wait for me. He waved and said, "Hi there," so I went over to speak to him.

"Bakers bake and bankers bank," the old man grumbled. "So could someone please tell me why gardeners don't garden?"

I suggested, "When you find one that does, better be nice to him."

"Guess that's the secret," he replied with a little laugh, then did a double take as I got closer and said, "Oh, you're not him. I was wondering..." He chuckled, more with embarrassment than humor. "This is terrible. Lived right next door for two years and don't even know their name."

"Delancey," I said.

"Oh."

I showed him my badge but put it away while he was still

trying to focus on it, told him, "You don't know them very well, eh?"

"No," he said emphatically. "What's wrong?"

"Mr. Delancey was murdered two days ago."

"No! My God! Really? What kind of a world is this getting to be?"

"Certainly not gentler and kinder," I said. "You didn't see much of your neighbors, eh?"

"Well no, not lately. Used to see him going and coming all the time—all hours of the day and night, I might add. She's a pretty little thing but I haven't seen her in months. Used to see her, at first, out in the back yard once in a while." He cocked an eye at me. "Sunbathing. In a teeny bikini. Let me tell you... but no, I think she left some time back. Used to talk a little bit back and forth across the fence. Him, no. Never looked left nor right, always seemed in a hurry. I worry about that place. Kids could break in there and raise hell, maybe burn it down, maybe mine with it. He's dead? So what's going to happen to the place?"

I told him, "Maybe it will get a nice young family with dogs and kids."

He said, "Oh no! I don't like dogs. Not right next door!"

"Kids and cats then," I suggested, and went on my way.

"I don't want kids right next door either!" he yelled after me.

It was getting to be a hell of a world, yeah. Gentler and kinder? Huh-uh. Not even right next door.

I HAVE a friend who operates a small travel agency. She had helped me before, I figured maybe she could again. The suitcases on Toni's bed bore the remains of old Eastern Airlines baggage checks. Wasn't much of a clue, but people do often have favorite airlines so I hoped it might narrow the search just a bit.

It did.

We found her under her real name on a flight to Washington leaving LAX at midnight, and the search required only about ten minutes. It cost me a future dinner date but what the hell.

I marked my mind for a midnight intercept at LAX and went on to Malibu, got there shortly past eight o'clock.

Dostell wasn't at home but his lady was. Didn't want to let me in the house but I insisted, kicked the door off the safety chain and caught her a glancing blow in the process. So, hell, she was surly and rubbing her butt while threatening to kill me in various terrible ways as I shook the place down looking for Frankie boy. I wondered why men like Dostell tolerated women like this one, decided maybe the aggravation was the only thing that kept him feeling alive. She had a mouth on her that could wither hardened felons and a vocabulary to match. Besides which, she liked to get right in your face and talk into your tonsils with every muscle in her body.

Finally I sat her down hard in a soft chair and dared her to bounce off of it. I think she was falling in love with me, kept rubbing her hip and wanting me to look at what I'd done to her, daring me to do it again and even suggesting other ways I'd better not hurt her.

Now this one I could see with a George Delancey maybe. Except I think that men like Delancey do it mostly in the mind— and when it does get beyond that level, they prefer the sweet, submissive, frightened women, not dragon-mouths like this one. Anyway, I had this gal's number. She fed on her own anger, not physical abuse from another. She could probably get off all alone on a desert island with no one to hear her but the seagulls if she could just keep worked up long enough.

I wasn't about to feed her, so I went outside and waited for Dostell in the car. Good thing, too, or I might have missed him entirely. I recognized his Ferrari lurching along the coast highway just uprange, saw it nose into the embankment and grind to a rest. The traffic was heavy and there were four lanes of it at that point but I managed to get over there without getting killed and tried to pull him out of the car. Couldn't do that; he was limp as a dishrag and I couldn't open the door widely enough because of the oncoming traffic.

He was as high as it's possible to get and remain alive—and from the looks of things, that would not be for long. I doubt that he even knew where he was or who he was, certainly not who I was.

"This is crazy, Frank," I told him. "You shouldn't be driving in this condition."

His speech was badly slurred and the words just barely recognizable but he seemed to be working at a semi-coherent message and trying desperately to get it across. "Shot me up, man, that's too much—can't handle this—kill me, kill me—Jesus!—burning me up!—where's the hospital, man?"

"Who shot you up, Frank? Who did it?"

This guy was collapsing from the inside out, as though muscle by small muscle was hanging out the do not disturb sign and going to sleep. Apparently he'd already lost the bladder muscles and peed his pants. His eyes were not tracking together and each movement of the head was a jerky, mechanical overshoot.

I worked at him for a minute or two, knowing all the while that it was no use. If the mind inside was functioning at all, the thoughts were finding very little resonance in the brain cells required to express them.

"Who did this to you?"

"Told 'em better. He no no no. I would no no."

"Frank! Try to focus! You're overdosed! Who did it?"

"She would say say. See? We no no no. Oh shit, man, shit man!"

"Did you see Nicky?"

"Nicky no no no. See he be he be. I no no no no."

I could not even hold him upright in the seat any longer. He was just a bag now, a skin covered bag with nothing but liquid inside seeking its flow back to the sea.

I stepped back and let him ooze away, closed the door to at least contain him to some measure, then I went back to tell his woman.

"Frank's car is just up the street. He's in big trouble. Better call the medics."

She gaped at me, all the anger turned off as though by a switch. "What's wrong?"

"Looks like an OD. Better hurry, he's fading fast."

She cried, "Oh my *God!*" and ran for the telephone.

I called after her, "Then I think you'd better get lost. Climb into a hole somewhere and pull it in over you."

"My God, why?"

"Whoever did it to him could feel the need to do it to you too."

"What are you *saying?*"

"A pile of people are dead, kid. And the pile is still growing. Do you know anything about Frank's business?"

She wildly shook her head. "We never talk about that."

"Call the medics," I said tiredly, and went out of there.

A police cruiser was parked behind the Ferrari when I went by, beacon flashing, so I knew that help would be on the way very shortly.

But I knew also that Frank Dostell was beyond help.

They say, live by the sword and you'll die by it.

This guy had died by the needle.

CHAPTER

TWENTY-SIX

I CONFRONTED Cherche in her private sex parlor and told her, "We've hit the bottom line here, old friend, so your life probably depends upon how well you can forget your vow of discretion and get down to raw truth. I've called a bomb squad out here. They'll be arriving any minute and you've got to fully cooperate with them. This place could be wired for destruction and I'm guessing the timing would be midnight while the party is in full swing. Meanwhile I want you to get everybody out and keep them out until it's declared safe. Are you following me?"

Her eyes were looking a little wild but the mental composure was still in place as she replied, "My goodness, darling, what a terribly devious mind you must have. Why would someone want to blow up my beautiful home?"

"Well it won't be a disgruntled neighbor," I assured her. "Sorry, darling, but you've been very badly used by some highly unscrupulous people."

"I feared such," she declared quietly. "Is it Nicky?"

"Sure it's Nicky," I confirmed. "It's also the PowerTron trio and Angélique and Thomas Chase and maybe two or three other determined conspirators. It's all centered right here, Cherche my love, and that makes your joint ground zero. They've already built one crater to cover the lunacy. I doubt they'd hesitate to bury it all right here. So clear this place out, and do it quickly. Nobody packs, nobody pauses to refresh the makeup—got it? Get 'em all out. I'll meet you outside."

She got it, and she went out quickly to spread the word.

I picked up the telephone and called the FBI. Took a couple of minutes to get through to Special Agent Browning and he came on angrily.

"Don't you ever rest, Copp?" he growled.

"Depends on what you call rest," I told him. "I need some info and I need it down, dirty, and quick. Do you have Toni Delancey under surveillance?"

There was just the briefest sense of indecision before he replied, "No, we've lost contact."

"Me too," I said, "but I think I've got a fix on her. She's booked out of LAX at midnight, Eastern flight to Washington. In case I don't get there in time..."

He said, "Thanks, appreciate the tip. What else do you have?"

"Frank Dostell is dead, I think."

Another brief pause, then: "Okay. Where is he?"

"Last I saw, he was dying behind the wheel of his Ferrari in Malibu with a cop looking on. Looked like an OD."

"With a little help, maybe."

"Seems that way, yeah. Call the L.A. police, they can update you."

"Okay. What else?"

"What'd you find out about your safe house?"

"Simple timing device. Blast was centered in the crawl space under the house. They used enough TNT to blow up ten just like it."

"Overkill."

"Yes, to make damned sure. I'm pissed about this, Joe."

"You need to be."

"Yes. If it turns out that you're involved..."

"I'm not."

"... there'd be egg all over my face, and that would piss me too."

"Wouldn't blame you. To tell the truth, I'm just a bit pissed myself. Someone has been screwing me over, and I mean with a royal twist. Level with me, my life could depend on it. Has Toni Delancey been working with you?"

"No."

"That's the dead level."

"It's dead level."

"Someone in the woodpile, Browning, knew about your safe house."

"Obviously."

"I mean before that. Either Toni knew or Nicky knew. I need to know which it was."

"When you find out, share it with me."

I said, "I'm betting on Toni."

"Sounds like an interesting logic, Joe, but I don't have time to pursue it right now. Have another death on my hands."

"Yeah?"

"Yeah. Special Agent Vasquez bought it a while ago."

I said, "Damn! The numbers are all coming down, aren't they?"

"Looks like it."

"How'd he go?"

"Shot in the head from behind. I'd had him on Toni Delancey, Joe."

I said, "Well dammit . . . !"

"Yeah. Keep in touch, will you?"

"I'll try," I promised. "See you at the airport maybe."

"Maybe," he said, and hung up.

I went in and tore Cherche's boudoir apart. Looked in every drawer, searched every surface, under every cushion and even under the mattress, behind every painting and inside every vase and light fixture.

Found many interesting things but left them all exactly as they were, got the hell out of there quick.

The joint deserved to blow.

Old friends or no, that place needed burying.

I STAYED around to assist the bomb squad in what small way they would allow. Told them about the earlier blow in Brentwood Park and they had a telephone conference with the people who'd investigated that one, started their search beneath the house. Basements are a rarity in Southern California and this house was no exception. The foundations were about four feet off the ground, though, so the crawl space was pretty good and these guys knew their business. Took them less than thirty minutes to locate four different bundles of dynamite wired to a single timer, less time than that to defang it and get it all out of there.

The sergeant in charge of the squad showed me the timer— set for midnight, as I'd suspected—and told me that any one of the dynamite bundles would be enough to blow the place to kingdom come. I made arrangements to meet with him the next day and sign a statement. His men made a thorough sweep of the house and were on their way by ten o'clock.

Cherche wanted to cancel the evening's activities, but I prevailed upon her to pick up and go on as though nothing out of the ordinary had happened there. She also agreed to telephone Nicky and invite him to a "special party" in her apartment at eleven-thirty, after which I took the phone and spoke to him.

"Hi Nicky, it's Joe Copp. Wanted to let you know that I'll be at the party, and maybe I'll have a little surprise for you."

"If it is what I am thinking, Joe..."

I said, "Yeah, you got it. Think I've found your missing property."

"Why don't you just bring it over here."

"Can't do that because it's not in my hands yet. I've arranged to pick it up at midnight."

"Perhaps we could pick it up together."

"Wouldn't work that way," I told him. "It's very delicate business. I'll get it and bring it straight to Cherche's."

"Why can't you just bring it straight to my apartment?"

I said, "No, I prefer neutral ground for this transaction."

"Transaction?"

"I don't work for free, Nicky."

"How much will it cost me to ransom my own property?"

I said, "You're looking at it all wrong. No ransom involved. Call it a finder's fee. Bring ten thousand U.S. Bring cash."

"This is highly important to me, Joe. Suppose..."

"It's important to both of us," I agreed. "Suppose what?"

"Why don't you let me send Ilyitch to back you up."

"No way," I said. "Sorry, I have to do this my way. I want you and Ilyitch and the other boys at Cherche's by eleven-thirty. I'll be in touch by telephone and when Cherche tells me you're there, I'll go ahead with the pickup."

"You are quite determined in this."

"You got it."

"Very well. But let's make an alternative plan in case our meeting goes astray."

"It won't," I assured him. "I'll be there shortly after midnight."

"But just in case, Joe. One could experience a traffic accident, a flat tire, these things happen. So as to not leave me in suspense...can we not say that we will meet elsewhere at a given time should the first meeting fail?"

I said, "Okay. If we don't connect at Cherche's, meet me at two o'clock in the lobby of the Beverly Hilton."

"Could we not just set it up that way at midnight?"

"Huh-uh. I'll have to know exactly where you're at before I go for the pickup. I trust Cherche to tell me where you're at."

Nicky was a bit dissatisfied with those arrangements but I left him no alternative. I also wanted something else from him.

"Now let's talk about Angélique. I want to know exactly what was the last thing she said to you."

"I don't understand, Joe. What does Angélique have to do with our arrangement?"

"Maybe nothing, maybe everything. I don't know exactly what I might be walking into, see, and I don't want to blow this thing because of some simple misunderstanding. The last thing she said to you."

"I believe it was 'good night,' Joe."

"Just before that."

"Let me see...she said that she would be in touch."

"About what?"

"Nothing in particular."

"She wasn't trying to work anything on your behalf?"

"I don't understand what you are getting at."

"You dropped her off in Brentwood Park at about two o'clock. You watched her enter a white cottage with brick planters. Was she going into that house to accomplish some task for you?"

"Not that I would know about."

"Did she tell you why she wanted to be dropped there?"

"No."

"You weren't even curious about it?"

"Perhaps I was curious. But one does not question a lady about her late night appointments."

"Was she carrying anything?"

"Carrying? In her arms?"

"Arms, hands, whatever. Was she taking something into that house?"

"You place me in a bad position, Joe."

"Not nearly as bad as the one I'm in. What did she take in there, Nicky?"

He paused for perhaps ten seconds before replying, "We had spent the evening searching for a rather infamous character who..."

"Dostell?"

"Yes.When we discussed this earlier, I felt rather constrained from speaking freely to you of this matter, but... is it tremendously important to you?"

"I think it is," I told him.

"Very well. The search for Dostell was on the behalf of Angélique. She desired very much to find him and to purchase something from him. We found him. She asked me to effect the purchase on her behalf. I did so. Then she asked me to drop her at Brentwood Park."

I said, "Let's be sure I have this straight. It was Angélique, not you, who made the buy from Dostell."

He replied, "I, on her behalf."

"Who put up the money?"

"Angélique gave me the money."

"How much?"

"Two hundred dollars."

"So you bought the stuff and gave it to her."

"Yes."

"And she had it with her when she left you in Brentwood Park."

"That is correct."

I said, "Thanks, you're a prince. See you at Cherche's."

I hung up and told Cherche, "He'll be here. For a while, anyway. But if this guy starts getting antsy and thinks up a reason to leave before midnight, maybe we'll know a lot more about cousin Nicky than he's dared to tell us."

Cherche was very distressed by that.

"I would have staked my life on Nicky," she quietly commented.

"Well don't write him off yet," I suggested. "Let midnight tell the tale."

"Very well," she said. "But if he tries to leave early, I feel that I might wish to kill him myself."

I almost believed she meant it.

I guess she did mean it.

I asked her, "How long has Alexandra been with you?"

"Quite some time," she replied absently, the mind obviously still playing at Nicky's throat.

"Before or after Angélique?"

"What do you mean? Oh. I found her months before Angélique found me. Is it important?"

Important enough, yeah.

The theory of the case was closing on itself fast, maybe too fast. At least I was in the saddle now and riding hard.

CHAPTER
TWENTY-SEVEN

I "BORROWED" Alexandra to keep me company at the airport. Working on a hunch, see, and thinking I might need an extra set of eyes to keep everything in sight. She was good company too. There'd been a chemistry between us from the beginning, besides which she was smart and observant. Took us half an hour to get to LAX, even at that hour of the night, and I used the time to satisfy some questions that still remained in my mind concerning Cherche's operation.

I asked her, "How does it work for a guy like Nicky Gudgaloff? Did he actually buy into the corporation?"

She replied, "Oh yes. There is no other way, really. Once in, though, the stockholder can distribute his dividends however he chooses."

"Gift certificates?" I asked with a grin.

"Subject to certain limitations," she said soberly. "He couldn't send a dividend to skid row, for example."

"No packages for the needy, eh?"

"Not that kind, no. These are usually business packages, Joe."

I said, "Suppose I was a stockholder. And I had certain dividends to collect. So I pick you up and we're driving about town in my limousine. We bump into a business acquaintance. I want to impress him. So I give you to him for the night. Would that be kosher?"

"To a point," she replied.

"What point?"

"It's more or less up to the girl, at that point."

"She could refuse?"

"If she felt uneasy about the situation, yes."

"But the pressure is on her to please the stockholder, isn't that true?"

"To a point, yes. Cherche is most careful, though, to educate the girls about certain dangerous situations and how to avoid them. She is really very protective of her employees. The final decision is always theirs."

"Have you ever had a situation like I just hypothesized?"

"Similar, yes."

"For example."

"I have gone to parties with one man and departed with another. Or I have gone with one and ended with several."

"You aren't afraid of those?"

"Depends. Generally, Joe, we are treated very well by our stockholders, with total respect. And you develop a relationship with some that furthers your sense of security."

"Like Nicky."

"Nicky is always the gentleman. He has never placed a girl in a dangerous situation."

I said, "But, generally speaking, these guys—stockholders—

can pass you girls around to whoever they please."

She replied, "Well, that is the beauty of it. For them. Each man who joins the corporation becomes like a sultan with his own private harem. He can dispense favors that few men alive today have at their disposal."

"Quite a business advantage, then, I would guess."

"From what I have seen, yes."

"Nicky has done a lot of that."

"Oh yes."

"Could he, say, set up a party on his own turf, have a number of girls attending?"

"He does so frequently. Nicky is one of our major stockholders."

"And the girls all respect him?"

"Oh yes. Nicky is a doll."

Well I didn't know about that. But a certain scenario was setting into my head. I asked, "Has he thrown private parties in Cherche's apartment?"

She gave me a sharp look and said, "We're getting rather specific, aren't we?"

I explained, "Cherche hired me to protect her best interests. I'm trying to do that. I know about all the hidden microphones and concealed television cameras in her apartment. I'm just trying to put together now an understanding of how they might be employed. You told me the other night that video parties have been arranged. Would that be part of that?"

"Could be," Alexandra replied quietly.

"Could be or has been?"

"I don't know if I should be..."

"I'm working for Cherche too, dammit."

She showed me a smile; said, "Did you know that she is planning to make you an offer no sane man would refuse?"

"What's that?"

"She wants to keep you on annual retainer as a security consultant, check out prospective stockholders and that sort of thing. Opportunity of a lifetime, Joe."

I said, "That would be like hiring a diabetic to run a candy store. Don't think I could take the heat, kid. It's an offer I could refuse."

"You ought to give it some thought, at least. Cherche is a very generous employer."

"Thanks," I said, "but I'm a man who knows his limitations."

She laughed softly. "I do believe that you are a hopeless square, Joe."

"Hope so," I said.

"Yes."

"Yes what?"

"Nicky has used the apartment for parties. Several times."

"Did the participants know about being on candid camera?"

"Oh yes. Cherche is very careful about that."

"So why is it all so hidden?"

"The idea is to be non-intrusive, not secretive. Helps the inhibited relax and get into the spirit."

"But each participant can buy a video?"

"Only the stockholder may order videos."

"But as many copies as he wants?"

"Yes."

"Has Nicky bought videos?"

"Yes."

The scenario was developing nicely, yes.

We reached the Eastern terminal at eleven-fifteen and I called Cherche at eleven-thirty. "Is he there?" I asked her.

"Nicky is just now arriving, Joseph."

"In full force?"

"In two cars, yes."

So it was all set.

The next half-hour should cast the scenario in concrete.

I PLACED Alexandra in the cocktail lounge in a position with an unobstructed view of all passengers arriving in the gate area, instructed her to watch for familiar faces, then I went on to meet an arriving flight from Washington due in at 11:45.

This was part of the hunch I was working. It had seemed a bit too easy to get that departure line on Toni, under her legal name and all. If she had set it up that way as a decoy, then maybe also she was the consummate operative I'd suspected her to be, selecting a decoy that would allow a sudden switch at the last moment, should it be necessary. LAX is one of those modern airports where individual airlines have their own separate terminal buildings. It is not easy to move from one to the other.

And I had a hunch about the 11:45 flight from Washington.

They were posting the flight to arrive on time, at a gate at the opposite side of the hub from which the midnight flight was scheduled to depart.

I got over there at 11:40, joined a crowd of fifty to sixty people waiting to greet the flight, tried to be as inconspicuous as possible while scanning the faces of those assembled there.

A noisy group of teenagers were part of the crowd, several obvious family groups as well, but most of the greeters appeared to be individuals waiting to meet someone. I got no whiff of Toni in that. The other flight would start boarding at 11:45 so I didn't want to devote too much time to checking out my hunch, was about to write it off and go to the other side when the incoming plane rolled up to the gate a few minutes early and the passengers immediately began deplaning.

So, what the hell, I gave it a few more minutes and hung around out of respect for my quivers.

It was the usual scene at such moments, weary travelers moving through the gate and searching the crowd for familiar faces, that crowd thronging about the exit point and also anxiously scanning every new face that appeared—delighted exclamations, smiles, tears, embraces, shy looks as people paired off or grouped off and moved on toward the baggage area.

My quivers leapt to full alert about halfway through all that when a whitehaired man of military bearing moved through the gate and started along the exit ramp. I had never seen Gordon Maxwell before, nor even a photo of him, but if this was not a retired brigadier general then I had never seen one—man of about fifty-five, vigorous and erect, tailored and coiffed for Wall Street, carrying a light hanging bag suspended from the shoulder.

One of the "kids" detached from the group of teenagers and stepped forward to take his hand.

It was Toni, yeah, but it required a good eye and an imaginative leap to identify her. A very expert use of cosmetics had all but neutralized the effects of her beating, except for a slightly puffy eye and lip.

She looked just like the other kids, in dress as well as demeanor—and I would bet dollars to doughnuts that she could alter herself again in a few seconds inside the ladies' room.

They moved aside from the flow of traffic to embrace in greeting—it seemed a rather warm embrace—then Toni produced a manila envelope from beneath her jacket.

That is when I made my move.

I closed immediately, grabbed the envelope, told them, "I'll have to detain you both."

Toni was mad as hell.

"You have no authority!" she cried.

I unbuttoned my coat to reveal the hardware at my waist, told her, "All I need, kid. I am licensed by the state of California to investigate crimes and to halt criminal activity by deadly force if necessary. Please don't make that necessary."

She was still mad as hell.

The PowerTron chairman just looked very sad.

I escorted them to the cocktail lounge and told them, "Be good and stay put until I get back, maybe I'll return your envelope and you can both go on about your business."

Then I collected Alexandra and we went on to check out the midnight flight.

I was feeling a bit sad, myself, about the whole thing.

NICKY'S "BLACK BOOK" was in the envelope, yeah, along with a page-by-page translation into English. As I'd already suspected, it was a record of his many "business contacts and compromising events beneficial to his mission in this country—very little to do with espionage but quite a bit with business advantages and arrangements, insider trading and the like, all the dirty tricks common to the capitalist creed now avidly sought by a nation just beginning to emerge from nearly a century of economic isolation and hardship.

The notes contained some pretty good avenues for blackmail, too, in unscrupulous hands—enough so that many highly placed individuals in both government and industry might shiver and shake over the prospect.

Shiver and shake enough, maybe, to produce much of the insanity that had come down during this week of horror, but the mere presence or absence of that book could not account for it all; it was merely a player among players, if my scenario was accurate, and would be seen ultimately as little more than a record of insanity, not the producer of it.

Alexandra told me that she had seen a familiar face enter the gate area. "His name is John Woodman," she said. "He knows Angélique. And he knows me."

"This the same guy planned the party for tonight?"

"Uh-huh. Close to Cherche. Big stockholder, but no portfolio."

"What does that mean?"

"All his stock is gratis."

"Why?"

"Influence."

I said, "Okay," and we went to find John Woodman.

It was five minutes before twelve, so I took a moment en route to call Beverly Hills.

"Is he still there?" I asked Cherche.

"Oh yes, darling, and quite comfortable. You see? I knew that my instincts were true."

I said, "Okay," and went on, hoping that my instincts were as true.

We looked around the gate area and found it almost deserted, most of the passengers boarded and only a handful of hangers-on peering through the windows to watch the plane depart.

I asked Alexandra, "Your man not here?"

She said, "No," and neither was mine—and I had a sudden shiver that sent me hurrying back toward the lounge.

We were about twenty paces out when Alexandra cried, "There he is!"

It was both her man and my man, he was carrying a trench coat draped across a forearm—and it was the wrong forearm.

It was also one of those frozen moments when you have the whole picture in view and wonder why you had not seen it much earlier, superimposed by the mind over the visual cortex which is also displaying the physical reality with Toni and Maxwell in the background like immobile targets in a shooting gallery and almost as close, a killer with a concealed, silenced pistol raised in the foreground—and you just cannot move the hand fast enough, it is all dreamlike slow-motion and you are working against some invisible restraining medium—then suddenly the gun was in my hand and banging away.

It sent three quick shots into that posing figure and flung it on into the lounge, the silencer-equipped pistol falling to the tiles outside and bouncing along wrapped in the trench coat.

Maxwell, ever the soldier of honor, leapt to his feet and shielded Toni with his own body as I scanned around in firing stance seeking another possible shooter.

But there was only the one—the worst thing to climb out of a cesspool, a kinky fed—Cherche's John Woodman and my Special Agent Theodore Browning, both under the same hat—and this one had died by his own game.

I called over to Maxwell, "Relax, General, it's all over now but the debriefing."

And so it was.

CHAPTER
TWENTY-EIGHT

IF THE human experience could be reduced to a basic exchange in which somehow we all could speak nothing but the truth to one another, then I suspect that a good many of our troubles would disappear. Certainly it would make a policeman's job much easier, because basically a cop has to proceed on the assumption that everyone is lying all the time and that he must determine his truths independent of what anyone may be saying to him. Realistically we know that not anyone lies all the time, but also that most anyone will lie some of the time, and sometimes for reasons that have nothing whatever to do with concealing a crime.

My big problem throughout this investigation lay in the fact that most everyone, even friends and lovers, had lied to me at least part of the time. That left me in the position of having to constantly build and rebuild a logic that would sort out the truths from the fictions yet use them all in an attempt to understand the moving forces behind it all.

I had not done so well at that.

In the defense of my policeman's intellect and instincts, though, please let me point out that there were many moving forces at work here and often at cross-purposes to one another. Many of them had been at play long before I joined the game, some others joined with me, still others came along as a direct consequence of my confused attempts to grab hold.

As I have stated earlier, Cherche was at the hub of it all—and even she became a confusion factor with her strong predisposition to shield her clients from public embarrassment—also because of her irrepressible romanticism and tendency to invent delightful fiction as a means of explaining an inexplainable world.

The intrigue did not begin with Theodore Browning—also know as John Woodman—but he was at the periphery of it when it all began and I choose to believe that he simply became swept into the vortex and had to start shooting his way out of it.

Special Agents Mathison and Vasquez had been in it with him.

Browning—as Woodman—was the inside man, setting up contacts through Cherche's operation for their double sting adventures and hovering over Nicky's coattails like a hungry seagull watching a fisherman for scraps of bait. He was really a hell of an effective cloak and dagger man, and he would have been a credit to the FBI if he had not grown so cynical and disaffected by the greed he must have experienced all around him—that's my guess, anyway—and decided to save a little for himself.

He saw guys like Putnam and Delancey feathering their nests with taxpayers' dollars—and God knows how many others—as well as the gentlemen stockholders of Cherche's Beverly Hills

Club wheeling and dealing in favors with illegal drugs as well as illegal women, a whole wide range of both personal and corporate "anything goes" corruption to boggle the police mind, and probably knew that he could not do a hell of a lot about it. So, okay, he joined it.

That is forever a hazard for the good cop, the smart cop who cares. Care becomes frustration and turns into cynicism and then into whatever else is available.

Browning and crew found quite a bit of availability. They found it all—from industrial secrets to national secrets—sex, drugs, pornography, blackmail—they found it all. And they decided to exploit it all.

They'd played it cool and cautious and were doing okay until Putnam and Delancey began having trouble maintaining their own merry-go-round of forbidden sex and expensive drugs. That was another movement. These guys had it all, but it was never enough. One pleasure fed on the next until they'd reached a point where it was all about to come tumbling down around them.

And it was their misfortune to then become impacted by still another movement, the rapid decline of Tom Chase. Tom had never been more than a very junior partner of their triad of coke, women, and secret deals. But he proved to be the most vulnerable to a destructive cocaine addiction and the least able to support such an addiciton.

As another cross-purpose, Tom had also forged links with the Browning-Mathison-Vasquez trio, so his meteoric decline was a matter of consternation for this group also.

The kinky feds were by this time so enmired in the network that vibrations in any part of it were felt immediately in every part.

Tom had gone to Putnam to demand a larger share of illicit profits, but Putnam evidently was savvy enough to know that this would be an ever-growing need. He was also savvy enough, I presume, to know that the pressures of the addiction would be stronger than Tom's sense of friendship or loyalty—so surely he could see the handwriting on that wall. Apparently he elected to shut Tom down at that point and began laying plans to shut him down entirely. He got in touch with Browning and suggested that something had better be done about Chase, and soon.

Tom was not that big a dummy either, whatever his weaknesses. He reacted by coming to me and dragging me into it in the hope that he could get some damning evidence to hold over the others. But then Browning struck and effectively took Tom out of play, protecting the whole network by declaring Tom an endangered witness and secreting him in the safe house until a more permanent solution could be found. I don't have all the particulars of that yet. Possibly he managed to convince Tom that he was acting in friendship because, remember, I had to slug Tom to take him out of there.

But then something got screwed up, I was not stopped in time, so I became another moving force via my burglary of the consulate and the liberation of Nicky's incriminating records.

Maybe Browning panicked, especially after my run-in with Mathison, and everything shifted into high gear. He either knew or surmised that I had taken something valuable and possibly damning from the consulate, and the rest became preordained. He had to minimize the damage. So he went after everyone, even close associates.

He or Vasquez killed Putnam and Delancey.

The mystery of my Smith & Wesson as the murder weapon remains a mystery, but I can offer an educated guess as explanation. I believe that either Browning or Vasquez had been stationed outside Toni's apartment the night that we surprised Mathison inside. We were followed when we left there—or else we were followed from the consulate—and they had us in their sights from that moment on. At some point after Toni left me stranded in the mountains, they found my gun while searching Toni's car—and maybe that is what inspired the fast move against Putnam and Delancey. They killed the two with my gun then planted it back in Toni's car, not even worried about recovering it themselves because I'd already confessed to the Mathison shooting and they knew that the ballistics evidence would tie me to Putnam and Delancey also. I feel that both men were already dead at the time that I was removed from the Soviet car just a few miles away—and that could explain why they waited to make their move on me at that point.

They were also the ones behind the submachine gun in the freeway shooting moments later, going for me but not at all squeamish about taking out three fellow agents in the bargain. I believe that those three were probably straight and that Browning merely used them in quick reaction to get me "in hand." In the grave was what he'd meant, and he'd damned near succeeded.

I can only guess as to the bombing of the safe house. Maybe Browning had thought to string Tom along and learn as much as possible from him, either decided that he'd gotten it all or that Tom was simply too dangerous alive—and of course the bombing would play well with the endangered witness idea. At any rate, he was the one who wired the place for destruction, timing it to coincide with a shift-change at seven A.M. and intending to take out everyone who'd been assigned to guard Tom Chase in that house. I learned later that he got only one of them, the guy I left lying there. That one had relieved the night watch thirty minutes early and his partner was delayed in traffic, got there too late to join the fireworks. But Browning had wanted them all, for sure, in his determination to eliminate any threat that could haunt him later.

Of course, when Tom escaped from my car, the only thing he

had in mind was to get back under Browning's wing. He reached him by telephone, and you know what happened then. Browning then reached Tom, tidying up the earlier sloppy attempt to erase any possible incriminating connection.

He killed Vasquez and Dostell for the same reason, then hoped to wipe out every possible connection with the network by removing Cherche's mansion and everything in it from the landscape.

I doubt that he'd made the connection of "Angélique" as Toni Delancey until very near the end. Apparently not even Tom Chase knew her true identity, and that brings us to the puzzle closest to my heart in all of this.

Toni Delancey, let me assure you, is truly something else. Some of what she'd told me about herself was true. She had served in the Israeli army, in the Mossad, and she had worked in the Washington intelligence community after returning to this country.

She's a tough little shit with strong ideals and guts to match. I have nothing but the highest admiration for Toni, even though she used me rather badly all the way through.

Gordon Maxwell had introduced her to George Delancey, had stood-in as her father and given her away at the wedding, and probably thought at the time that he had done something very nice for both of them.

Maybe that could have been true. But George was a kinky son of a bitch, always was, still would be if Browning had not straightened him out with a bullet, one of those guys who is all charm on the outside and nothing but sewage on the inside.

Didn't take Toni long to tumble to that.

Took her even less time to dissociate herself from it. By then, though, she'd learned enough to know that PowerTron itself along with her old friend Gordon Maxwell was in jeopardy because of her husband's manipulations of the company. Being

Toni, she went to Maxwell with the story; being Maxwell, he took instant action and sent Toni right back into the thick of the conspiracy in an attempt to develop intelligence that would shield PowerTron from government prosecution.

Through their connections in the intelligence community, they worked out the angle of penetration via Cherche. Since Toni actually was from Israel, it seemed an easy enough pose and yet one which would encourage Cherche to provide the maximum protection for Toni. I understand that about all that Toni ever did for Cherche was to ride around town with Nicky in his limousine and front his social contacts. He liked her, and she had all the social graces, made him look good. The association also served Toni's purposes as a good vantage point from which to discern the various connections of the "network."

She had never met Tom Chase until his panicky and therefore clumsy attempt to penetrate Cherche in his own interests. But of course she knew his name and reputation, therefore quickly recruited him to her purposes while he thought that he was recruiting her.

See, all the players had a game.

And that is mainly what drove me crazy for three days trying to separate it all out.

Toni's game had been a very direct one, to learn all she could about the network while gathering evidence to absolve Power-Tron when the crunch came. Maxwell's major concern was to identify every employee who was involved, and he'd moved quickly once the evidence narrowed it down to the triad, but not quick enough to anticipate the explosive developments that followed my entry into the thing.

Who beat Toni up?

Old pal Tom Chase did that. He'd been going a little crazy since his arrest, deprived of his accustomed massive ingestions of cocaine and suffering from severe withdrawal. Browning knew, of course, that Toni had been part of Tom's little game of intrigue and that she'd become involved with me, but I think he was largely in the dark about her and puzzled. On the other hand, Toni knew Browning only as John Woodman.

Cherche, however, knew exactly who he was and considered him a protective asset to her operation. When he called in a "dividend" and specifically asked for "Angélique" to deliver a few grams of cocaine, Cherche felt compelled to honor the request —and Toni departed on her date with Nicky already assigned to deliver for "Woodman" after delivering for Nicky.

She had not known that Tom Chase was being detained at that address in Brentwood Park. Browning himself had been standing at that doorway waiting to quickly admit her and take her back to Tom's bedroom. Possibly he'd sent the regular guards on some errand, or maybe he brought her in right under their noses while they enjoyed a coffee break in the kitchen or something. Whatever, he sent Toni to the bedroom with the cocaine and ordered her to "also relieve the boy's tensions," possibly as a test of some kind.

Apparently Toni failed the test and Tom angrily knocked her around some before Browning stepped in and pulled her out of there. He took her to Cherche's and dropped her at the gate, not at all worried about any compromise to his "safe house" because he already had it wired to blow at seven o'clock anyway.

It was the finale for Toni, though. When she reported the incident to Maxwell by telephone, he immediately ordered her out of there and set up the "staged withdrawal" which played itself to a standstill at the airport that night.

By then, and maybe thanks to me, Browning had put Angélique and Toni into the same body so he knew that she was a definite threat. He'd come there to kill her, and probably me too. I can almost feel sorry for the guy. By this time he was in so deep and there were so many loose ends flopping about the cesspool, he must have been at the very end of his tether and going a little wild himself inside.

After the shooting, I surrendered his ID and gun to the airport cops and explained that it was a simple apprehension of a murder suspect. For some reason, I guess they thought Browning's ID was mine because they handed it back to me and let me walk away after promising to make a full report downtown. I did that, of course, and cleared the whole thing to everyone's eventual satisfaction, but I waited a few hours to do that.

Had a date with Nicky, see, and I met him at the Beverly Hilton as promised. Gave him back his little black book but not the English translation—Maxwell had that—and I didn't bother to worry Nicky with knowledge of that. He was happy to get his "property" back, even insisted I take the ten grand although I had been kidding about that, and I heard later that he'd returned to Moscow the next day. Cherche is quite sad about that, but I'm sure she'll find another Nicky somewhere in the woodwork. As for Nicky himself, I guess I'll never know if he was buying coke for himself or trying to set up a diplomatic supply line to the Kremlin to grease some connections there, but the wonder of it has made something of a Kremlin-watcher of me; I keep looking for his name to surface in connection with purges or promotions and I'm betting on promotions. There is, after all, a whole new wind blowing across Mother Russia.

I guess those warm hours in front of the fire in that mountain chalet had not meant the same thing to Toni that they meant to me. She wants to live in Washington and play with cloaks and daggers. That's okay—life is more than a rose garden, after all. Toni is still very special to me, and I guess I will always think of her when I awaken in the night and the pillow beside me is bare. Course, that may not be happening too often in the future. I'm learning to take my special moments as they come, without trying to attach lifetime significance to them, and that is working out pretty good with Alexandra's help. I'm sure there will be someone after Alexandra, someone after that, someone after that.

Meanwhile I have a couple of tantalizing offers to consider and probably eventually reject, but I'm having fun thinking about them anyway. General Maxwell wants to bring me into his corporate setup, Cherche LaFemme into hers. Told Cherche she'd have to get out of the video business, too much insecurity there, but...

I'll probably just stay with my own.

I mean, what the hell, all I will ever be is a cop. It's enough.

11/91
#/90